BILLIE SWIFT TAKES FLIGHT

ISZI LAWRENCE

BLOOMSBURY EDUCATION

LONDON OXFORD NEW YORK NEW DELHI SYDNEY

To Felicity and Penny

With thanks to Air Transport Auxiliary Museum & Archive at Maidenhead Heritage Centre

BILLIE SWIFT
TAKES FLIGHT

BLOOMSBURY EDUCATION
Bloomsbury Publishing Plc
50 Bedford Square, London, WC1B 3DP, UK
29 Earlsfort Terrace, Dublin 2, Ireland

BLOOMSBURY, BLOOMSBURY EDUCATION and the Diana logo are trademarks of
Bloomsbury Publishing Plc

First published in Great Britain in 2021 by Bloomsbury Publishing Plc

A catalogue record for this book is available from the British Library

ISBN: PB: 978-1-4729-8817-1; ePDF: 978-1-4729-8807-2; ePub: 978-1-4729-8808-9

2 4 6 8 10 9 7 5 3 1

Typeset by Newgen KnowledgeWorks Pvt. Ltd., Chennai, India
Printed and bound by CPI Group (UK) Ltd, Croydon, CR0 4YY

To find out more about our authors and books visit www.bloomsbury.com
and sign up for our newsletters

CHAPTER ONE

It wasn't as though Billie Swift liked getting in trouble. If anything, she tried not to be in trouble. At the same time, being good didn't mean she stayed out of trouble. And being bad didn't mean she got into trouble. Some of the worst things Billie had ever done had gone unpunished. Like the time at the wishing well when she wished her brother would disappear forever. Equally, when Billie was the most honest, she was often punished. Like the time Mrs Ganderlilly asked if Billie liked her new hat. None of it made much sense to her.

This time, Billie knew that what she was doing was technically being naughty. She had put Susan, her favourite hen, in the basket of her brother's bicycle after she had come home from school and taken Susan with her to go plane spotting. She had done this for several complicated reasons.

1

Firstly, she didn't want to be home when her mother arrived back because she hadn't peeled the carrots. She hadn't peeled the carrots because she hadn't picked the carrots. She wasn't certain which of the rows of green plants in the back garden were the carrots that needed to be picked. She knew she must have been told but she hadn't been listening. She was worried she'd pick the wrong thing. That would be wasting food. You could go to prison for wasting food.

The whole situation was too much, so she had picked up Susan who had been perched on the stone bench and taken her up the hill behind the church. The hill was part of the manor house's estate, but away from the posh gardens and orchard. No one came up here. They were scared of the old gamekeeper who patrolled the grounds. Playground stories spread fast about him firing his shot gun at boys scrumping apples, and kidnapping and eating evacuees. Billie didn't voice her scepticism. It was her own place. She could relax, prop the bicycle against a tree and look down the hill towards the airfield to watch the planes land. There was always a rush of them arriving just before it got dark. They never flew at night. Only the Nazis flew at night.

Even before the war, the skies had been busy at White Waltham. The planes had circled the airfield enjoying the views of the rolling English countryside.

'Like flies round a corpse,' Mrs Swift would say, while shutting the windows to block out their engines.

When Billie was small, she had been scared of the noise. But knowing what made the terrible sound took away her fear. Her brother had told her a few of the names and, after she spilt cocoa on her father's reference books, he had let her keep his aircraft recognition guides in her bedroom. Billie would stare as hard as she could at the planes, mouthing their names over and over again. Soon, she knew more planes than anyone. This was a trick she used with people too, to less success. In church, she had focused on Mrs Hoggard's hat two rows in front, whispering the words 'Hoggard, Hoggard, Hoggard,' loudly under her breath. Mrs Hoggard and her children had avoided her ever since.

This year there were new planes for Billie to learn to recognise. Large bombers as well as the smaller fighters turned low over the tiny cottage where Billie lived. When she didn't know their official names, she nicknamed them things like Bumblebee, Spectacles, Crane and Growler. After school she would often go to the bookshop at Maidenhead train station and thumb through the air magazines until she was chucked out by the staff.

Billie could tell the difference between many types of plane while sitting in the cupboard under the stairs.

The cupboard was her family's version of the Anderson shelter. They had never bothered with getting a proper one, since they were expensive and air raids were few and far between in White Waltham. However, after a bomb had left a thirty-foot crater nearby, Billie's mother had upgraded from blankets under the kitchen table to the more sturdy (and more spidery) cupboard. Billie rather liked it and had taken to sitting in there with a candle and a book whenever her mother was looking for her.

Billie's mother wouldn't be looking for her yet. She was still on shift as an ambulance driver. Billie would be able to see Dr Bundock's car giving her mother a lift back from the hospital from her hillside vantage point. Once she had gone back, Billie would also return and claim that an escaped chicken had distracted her from doing the carrots.

What Billie hadn't factored into her plan was the sound of an engine cutting out. She hadn't even registered it properly; she was still looking down at the airfield, watching a Fairchild plane taxi into one of the hangars. The wind picked up. Susan fussed in her basket, clucking as she hunkered down.

The trees were clinging to their dry tatty leaves. They rustled noisily, masking the sound of a pilot somewhere

4

in the distance trying to restart an engine. An engine of a plane that was coming closer and closer to Billie's lookout point.

Suddenly, it felt like a cricket ball was spinning past her ear. There was a lack of noise, a heaviness that made Billie's stomach drop. Something was far too close and far too large. It didn't even make a proper whoosh overhead, nor did it whistle like a bomb. It passed so quickly it felt unreal.

Susan and Billie both clucked in shock.

Billie had often wondered what it would feel like to have a bomb drop on top of her and, for a split second, that was what she thought was happening. After all, there was no growl of an engine or fumes of exhaust. A branch from the tree she had propped the bicycle against cracked down next to her, the twigs whipping the back of her head. She thought she glimpsed the bullet shape of a bomb falling from above as she staggered to regain her balance, her feet sliding in the mulch. Only, bombs weren't so massive and they didn't have wings.

It was a Spitfire! Billie rubbed her head where the branch had hit her, watching the plane intently. It was out of control, coming in too low and too steep, clipping the tops of the trees on the hill. It wobbled as it descended, blown about by invisible gusts of wind. Its nose was up, as though it was trying to land, but it was nowhere near the airfield. It came in short, making an ill-advised dive for the field, just yards from Billie's lookout.

For a moment, Billie thought it was OK; all the wheels touched the ground as it tried to lose speed. Had it been on a smooth grass airfield it might have made it, but Billie knew that field. It was an ankle twister, full of flint rocks and rabbit holes. It sloped unevenly down towards the airfield. The Spitfire bounced a few times, as though it was trying to take off again. Each time, gravel and stones scraped and pinged against the fuselage. Then its nose tilted down. Billie gasped as she saw the plane tip up, like a gymnast doing a headstand. She thought for a moment that it was going to stay balanced on its nose but then it toppled forwards, landing upside down with a crunch. The only noise was the faint sound of its spinning wheels in the wind.

CHAPTER TWO

Billie stood staring in total shock. Over at the airfield, the Fairchild had made it inside the hangar. The roads were empty. The upturned Spitfire was silent. Susan had busied herself pecking at the ground next to the fallen bicycle. Billie didn't notice her hen. She was waiting for the pilot to come out of the plane. Hurry up. She wondered if he was all right. Perhaps he was hurt. What should she do?

She knew better than to go up to the plane. Things with engines could catch fire. She'd been instructed repeatedly at school that in an emergency her duty was to get adult help but the truth was, Billie would have preferred to catch fire than to ask strangers for help. She didn't know why. The thought of running up the hill to pound on the door of the manor house made

Billie shudder. She pictured knocking on the door, the butler's sneering face, her trying to explain, him telling her off for trespassing, or telling her mother where she'd been. She could ask at Burycourt farm which was on the other side of the road from the church. She didn't know the names of the land girls who worked there. Her mother called them ne'er-do-wells. She couldn't go to the farm with Susan anyway, they might think she'd stolen her from them. Or the vicarage! Just beyond the upturned plane was the red brick vicarage. The plane must have made a loud enough crunch as it flipped for them to notice... if the vicar was in.

She hesitated and thought she would have to go down herself.

BOOM!

The explosion wasn't the plane. She recognised it at once as a shotgun. She regularly heard the sound of pheasant hunts but those were always somewhere in the distance. This was so close that she actually jumped and slid in the mud.

'Who's there? You're trespassing!'

The man's voice was a growl and seemed to come from every direction. Billie scrabbled to her feet, her hands clutching the mud, and attempted to rescue the bicycle from underneath the fallen branch that had knocked it over. It was too heavy. Susan had made a beeline for the brambles. Billie abandoned the bicycle as the sound of crunching footsteps and the clinking of a gun being reloaded grew closer. She snatched at Susan, cutting her arm and tearing a hole in her sock as she plucked up the bird and pulled herself away.

She was in a panic. It felt as though she were running through treacle. Her stumbles felt so slow, her feet slipping on the leaves as Susan was trying to kick against her. Words of warning about the demon gamekeeper and his bloodthirsty wolf echoed through her mind. Low-lying branches whipped her as she barrelled through them. She reached the dry-stone wall of the church graveyard and dived for it, doing a sort of awkward cartwheel and landing on her side in the long, wet grass by the forgotten graves. She let go of Susan, who immediately scuttled off to shelter under a large yew tree. Billie pressed herself up against the wall to hide. She couldn't hear anything except her own loud gasps. Once she was able to breathe through her nose, she realised that it was nearly dark. Her mother would be home soon.

Trembling, she peeked her head over the wall. There was no one there, just the dark wood she'd run through. She daren't risk fetching the bicycle. As she chased

Susan around the yew tree she thought again of the Spitfire, but reasoned that the gamekeeper must have seen it. That's why he had been there, to look at the plane. He'd probably found the bicycle too.

Billie's plan to return home claiming to have had to catch an escaped hen turned out to be the truth by the time she got there. Her mother was saying goodbye to Dr Bundock as she walked up to the gate.

Mrs Swift took one hard look at her bedraggled daughter and sighed. 'I've told you a thousand times; I want you home before it starts getting dark.'

Billie tried to explain. 'Susan kept running away.'

'Put her back with the others and come inside...'

The others hens eyed Billie suspiciously when she returned with a rather roughed up Susan.

'She's alright,' Billie told them as they scuttled over to check she was one of them. For a horrid moment Billie thought they might fight, as they sometimes did when one had been out of the coop for too long. Fortunately, Susan scampered up the ramp and with a bit of coaxing by Billie, the others followed. She lowered the wooden latch and went back to the house.

Mrs Swift watched her daughter take off her filthy shoes and dump them unceremoniously by the back door.

'And since when have twigs been a fashion item?' She walked over and plucked them out of Billie's hair. As she did, she touched her face. 'Your cheeks are freezing, child. What have you been doing?'

Billie couldn't begin. It was too much to blurt out all at once. The woods. The plane. The pilot. The gun. The bicycle. Susan. The carrots. It all rushed to the front of her mouth and evaporated. Nothing could explain it all; nothing could make reason from her actions. Or inactions.

Mrs Swift didn't seem to notice her daughter's frustrated expression and carried on without pausing. 'Of course, a thoughtful daughter might have said, "Sod those chickens. I'll tidy the place up before my mother gets home."'

'Sorry.'

'If this year is anything like last, we are going to need more firewood. Perhaps you could go and get some kindling while you're out playing zoo keeper,' Billie's mother continued. 'Where did you find your escapee this time?'

Billie faltered for a moment. Her mother wouldn't believe Susan would have gone as far as Waltham Place. It was easier to be vague.

'Not far,' Billie lied.

'Next time, don't go chasing after her. If she gets run over it is her own fault. I don't want to lose both my children to this awful war.'

Billie's mother looked tired. The jar with the tea was out of the cupboard and no trace of lipstick remained on her lips. The decision to stay at home had been made. Billie knew telling her about the gamekeeper or the plane crash would make her go out, and that would make her furious. Besides, she'd tell Billie off for not explaining right away and losing Michael's bicycle. The longer Billie left it, the more impossible it was to tell.

The clock on the wall was fast, but it already said six thirty. Billie hurriedly climbed up, kneeling on the sink to reach the blackout curtain. It didn't budge unless you got it right at the top.

'Careful!' Billie's mother said, as she switched on the lights.

That was the last word she said that evening. They went through their routine. Billie's mum sat quietly reading the paper. Billie's father wouldn't be home until the weekend. Until then it was just the two of them, beans on toast, and the Home Service on the wireless.

Billie worried her mother could hear the thoughts in her mind. They were much louder than the radio burbling in the living room. Billie couldn't stop wondering if the pilot was injured. Had the gamekeeper found him? Was he dead? Could Billie have helped him in time?

Now it seemed obvious what she should have done. She should have put her hands up and called to the gamekeeper that there had been an accident. Together they could have run down the hill and helped the pilot. Anything was better than what Billie had actually done: run away. She'd fled like a miserable coward.

Billie didn't sleep well that night. There was no air raid warning, no thunderstorms keeping her awake or Nazi planes flying over. Just the buzzing in her ears. The impossible silence of the falling Spitfire and her own indecision. She kept telling herself that the gamekeeper would have spotted the crashed plane. But she couldn't be sure. If that pilot was dead, she had as good as killed him.

'That is the second time you've murdered someone, Billie Swift,' she murmured to herself. And she didn't much like it.

CHAPTER THREE

Billie sat down at the table.

'All that time out there and you've not found any eggs?'

Billie shook her head. 'Susan is upset.'

'We've seven hens, String-bean. No eggs is somewhat troubling.'

'But they follow Susan, don't they? She's top hen. Harris and Dowding usually lay at tea time. And Mountbatten copies them,' Billie suggested. 'Which leaves Alexander, Portal and Montgomery...'

'I should never have let Michael name them...' Mrs Swift stopped for a moment as she did every time Billie's brother came up in conversation.

'Maybe they are still moulting? Perhaps they don't like the shorter daylight,' said Billie, sagely.

'Eat your toast. Put some jam on if you must, but I'm saving the margarine.'

'I'm not hungry,' Billie said with a yawn.

'You're not allowed to be ill,' her mother said, sternly. 'I'll pick up the shopping. Can you post those?'

She pointed to a pile of letters next to the 'display only' margarine and leant over to kiss Billie on the head.

'Good girl.'

She left.

Billie wondered if she could just stay home. No one would know. But the chickens needed routine. Billie not going to school might upset them further.

Billie went next door to the post office. She eyed the posters in the window. The diagonal tape that had been placed across the glass made them hard to read. The pictures were of a smug-looking woman in various poses: sat doing her nails by an electric fire or gesturing with her thumb at a queue of shoppers. There was a poem too.

'The Woman Who Wouldn't said, "Queues
Are terribly hard on the shoes
But Black Market shopping
Is not. There's no stopping
Me shopping wherever I choose."

But all thanks to the women like You,
To the millions who Would and who Do,

Not selfishly spending,
But saving and mending
And working to see Britain through.

Billie wrinkled her nose at the limericks and felt jealous of the smug cartoon sat by the fire. However bad the 'woman who wouldn't' was, Billie felt sure even the 'woman who wouldn't' would have helped that pilot last night.

Could the pilot have survived all night trapped in his cockpit upside down? Doing handstands made Billie's eyes want to pop if she held them for too long. What if she went up to the plane, looked inside and his head had exploded? It would be too late to get help. And if she did get help, how could she explain being there, in a field on Waltham Place estate rather than in school?

Still, she needed to retrieve her brother's bicycle. She would go after school, she thought to herself. Anything to put off the moment when she'd discover a headless corpse. She turned and walked in the opposite direction towards the school gates, still holding her mother's letters in her hand.

Billie didn't have a school uniform but wellingtons certainly weren't allowed. She didn't even notice she was wearing them. Her head was elsewhere. Not so much 'in the clouds' as crashing towards the ground.

Mr Hart was holding open the door to the classroom for her. He was a posh man with a white moustache, tinted yellow through pipe smoke. He used to teach at a famous boarding school years ago. For some reason the children had nicknamed him 'Custard' though Billie didn't understand why. Their previous teacher, Miss Yates, had left to join the Wrens and Mr Hart had come out of retirement to teach what he called 'a ragbag bunch of young hoodlums'.

Now the evacuees had been moved back to London or been shuffled into a school in Maidenhead, the teachers were much less frantic. Mr Hart allowed entire afternoons for the class to go blackberry picking on September afternoons or, if the weather didn't allow, reading the Beano or Dandy comic books. Billie was aware that her education was another casualty of the war.

'A clodhopper in clodhoppers,' Mr Hart said.

'What's a clodhopper, sir?'

'Never you mind.'

One good thing about the lessons was that they were quiet. It was the lunchtime break Billie had difficulty with. That was when the other children insisted on talking to her. It wasn't that they picked on her; in fact, they often tried to be nice to her. The trouble was, they all wanted to be nice to her at the same time. Billie found it hard to cope. She often made an excuse to stay behind in the classroom. She'd rather tidy up than exhaust herself trying not to say the wrong thing or scream at them to shut up.

Before the war, she had gone home for lunch but as the evacuees had nowhere to go, the rules had changed.

Today, everyone stayed inside to avoid the rain. Billie's classmates had broken into smaller circles of friends. Two of the boys were punching each other on the arm. Some of the girls were restyling their hair. Billie sat at her desk. Motionless, like Susan when she saw a fox. The noise level gradually began to rise.

Billie hated the noise of people talking. She much preferred chickens, who only had five or six different noises. The excited clucking as they ambled towards food, the warning cluck when the crows flew over, the warning cluck when they saw a cat or fox, the squabble squawk, the proud crowing when they laid an egg and, Billie's favourite, the brooding murmur as Susan settled on her lap. Chickens managed to organise themselves perfectly using so few noises. Why did people make such a meal out of communicating?

The thing Billie really couldn't stand was people talking all at once. It was as though Billie was on a perfectly green lawn, her chin on her hands, looking into the grass and each voice was a tiny ant. Being in a room full of talking was, for Billie, like sitting with hundreds of ants climbing all over her shoes, her legs, her back, in her belly button, her hair... She could feel them everywhere. Itching. Tickling. It was too much. She couldn't focus. She couldn't think. It made her want to scream.

She got up from her desk and ran to the classroom wall. Leaning with her back against it, she slowly slid down, thinking about the cool on her back, not her classmates shrieking and playing. At least with her back to the wall, all the noise was coming in from the front and not all around her. She shut her eyes and tried to block it out.

'Are you alright?'

'Yes,' Billie lied, screwing up her face.

'What's happened to Billie?' said another voice.

'Is she mad?'

'Shall I get her some water?'

Not only were they talking, they were getting close. Breathing on her.

'Go away!' yelled Billie. She shouted it so loudly the boys stopped punching each other.

Someone grabbed her arm and pulled her up and away from the wall.

'LEAVE ME ALONE!' Billie shouted. 'Get off me!'

Billie opened her eyes and ran across the classroom to the door. There were scrapes of chairs and clatters as the children got out of the way.

'Ignore her, she only does it for attention.'

She opened the heavy door and stumbled out into the empty corridor. As the door swung back shut behind her, her heart rate slowed and Billie became aware of two things. Firstly, the calm drumming of rain on the roof and secondly the stinging in her forearm. She looked down.

By her wrist were her own tooth marks. To stop herself from yelling, she had bitten down her arm. She hadn't even noticed she'd done it.

Billie winced as there was a bloom of laughter from behind the classroom door. Probably about her.

Making friends was something that her mother wanted her to do. But she just couldn't. The other children didn't like the things she liked, they didn't want to do what she wanted to do and always asked stupid questions. They weren't like Susan who would happily peck at the ground while Billie copied out the silhouettes of enemy aircraft on her mother's favourite letter paper.

Where would Susan go now? Outside. Find somewhere to shelter from the rain.

CHAPTER FOUR

Billie ran down the side of the muddy playing field and dashed to the log store. It was open to the elements, having only three walls, but it was covered over with a big sheet of tin. The log supply was low so Billie could sit on top of it. Billie liked it in here. There were some amazing creepy crawlies. She knew she should go back to the classroom. Lessons would be starting soon. But she preferred it here. It was cold, it was wet, it was calm.

In the distance, a plane was taxiing to the runway, about to take off. Billie wasn't sure what it was, but it had more than one engine. It was loud. A Mosquito? She caught a glimpse of the machine roar over the distant trees, and saw she was right. The moment required a celebration and she felt in her cardigan pockets and pulled out her mother's post and two carrots. Feeling guilty about the envelopes, she stuffed them back in her pocket and ate one of the carrots.

'Hands up!'

Billie's head whipped round. A boy holding a shotgun was in the entrance of the wood store. He had an oversized raincoat, long trousers and boots, but he was definitely a boy. He was older than Billie but not by much. He wore a blue cap.

'Ha, scared you!' he said, lowering his gun and propping it up against the wall of the wood store. He busied himself with getting dry, and wrang out his cap, placing it next to Billie on the woodpile.

Billie suddenly recognised him. He had left school in the summer. He had a name like Jonny or Charlie though she couldn't remember it.

'What are you doing here?' Billie asked.

'Hunting for dinner.'

'Rabbits?'

'I thought the rain would cover any noise I made,' the boy sighed, 'but I think they are all sheltering. What are you supposed to be doing?'

'Geography,' Billie said.

'Bunking off?'

Billie ignored the question. 'Do you work for the RAF now?'

He laughed. 'No. I'm fourteen.'

'But you work on the airfield. I recognise the cap.'

'It's not an RAF airfield, stupid. It's the Air Transport Auxiliary. We are civilians.'

'But the planes are RAF planes,' Billie pointed out.

'Yeah, we deliver the planes to the RAF.'

'Why can't the RAF fetch their own planes?'

'If you hadn't noticed, there is a war on. They are a bit busy.'

'You've actually flown in them?' Billie asked.

'I haven't gone solo yet but they let me go along on a few flights.' His chest puffed a bit. 'You're Mrs Swift's daughter, aren't you?'

Billie nodded.

'Sorry to hear about your brother.'

It was more than Billie could bear to be reminded of Michael.

'Did you hear that a plane crashed last night?' Billie blurted quickly.

He blinked then said slowly. 'There wasn't an air raid last night.'

'No, it was a Spit, not Woof laugher.'

He burst into giggles. 'Woof laugher!'

'I meant Luftwaffe,' Billie smiled at her mistake.

He continued to laugh, 'I know... I know but you said...'

Billie grinned. 'Woof laugher?'

He convulsed with giggles again. He snorted like a pig and it was infectious. Billie was laughing too.

'Oh my, oh my…' He tried to catch his breath.

'But the Spitfire that crashed…' Billie prompted him. Maybe he knew what had happened to the pilot.

'How do you know about that?' He stopped laughing and frowned.

'Is the pilot alright?' asked Billie.

'You shouldn't even be asking!' He looked angry. 'How do you know about it?'

'Some boys were talking about it in the classroom,' Billie lied.

He picked up his gun. 'You are trouble. Careless talk costs lives.'

He marched back outside, forgetting his wet cap.

Billie picked up his cap. Inside the rim was stitched 'property of Tommy Hughes'. His reaction to her questions made Billie believe the pilot was dead. That must be why Tommy didn't want to talk about it. The pilot had died and she could have helped. She felt a cold chill somewhere near her heart that had nothing to do with her wet cardigan.

CHAPTER FIVE

It was still raining when she walked back, past her house and the post office and up the hill to the narrow gate near the graveyard.

She had no chicken with her this time. Overhead planes droned, slowly making their way towards the airfield. She stopped and looked as a Halifax bumbled in like a great fat gurgling baby, its four engines heaving to keep it in the air.

She reached the church and looked around for the gamekeeper. She took a shortcut, climbed over the fence, and jogged along the path to where she had stood yesterday, stopping like a frightened hare every time she heard a squirrel rustle in the leaf litter.

Looking down the hill she was confused to see that the field was now empty. No plane, no people, no pilot.

She would have questioned her memory had she not reached the freshly cracked branches that the plane had broken yesterday. The snapped wood shone white above the toppled bicycle. The bicycle that had been knocked over by those branches. The branches that had been broken by a falling Spitfire. The Spitfire that had crash landed in that field.

Where was the plane?

The anxious feeling was still with her when she went to bed that night. She tried not to imagine being trapped in a plane upside down. Waiting for someone to help.

It must have been as late as ten o'clock when she heard the door slam and her father walk into the hallway. His feet pattered up the stairs and her bedroom door creaked open.

'Cuckoo,' whispered the silhouette at the door. It creaked shut again.

Billie didn't know what her father did for the war effort. She knew he didn't fly planes or shoot guns but he didn't bring home extra rations or interesting looking papers either. Just a briefcase full of numbers and a tired face. She was lucky that this exhausted adult was safe for her to say hello to at weekends. Some children had had to move away from home and others' daddies never came back.

Her blanket felt heavier than usual. The air was cold. She could hear her parents' movements downstairs. Scraping chairs and muffled conversation.

She couldn't ask them about the plane of course. Then they would know she'd lied about the carrots and had taken Susan out of the chicken coop for no good reason. If they knew she lied so much they would realise what a bad person she was. They would know Michael not coming home was because she had wished it.

She rolled over and looked up at the ceiling. The whooshing of her blood in her ears sounded like the Spitfire had as it fell over her head towards the field. What if she had gone down the hill to help? She turned over. She had to find out what had happened to the pilot or she would never sleep again.

***

Billie did sleep of course. She woke up to the sound of the chickens squabbling. Her mother liked to be egalitarian when she fed them, which upset the pecking order. It made everyone unhappy.

Her father was coughing downstairs, moving slowly about.

Still in her nightgown, Billie slipped out of bed and gently opened the door to her room. She tiptoed across the corridor to her brother's room. The door handle was dusty to the touch. Checking to see no one was coming up the stairs, she eased open the door, just wide enough to let herself slip inside.

It smelt like an old book. Gradually her eyes became accustomed to the light that leaked in where the blackout curtain had slipped. All his things were still here. The stack of magazines, tin soldiers, and playing cards. She went to the wardrobe and took out grey slacks, braces, a shirt and his blazer. It was the same blue as the uniform Tommy wore under his raincoat.

She snuck back out of his bedroom, pulling the door to. Back in her room, Billie was glad she had thought to take his braces. The trousers wouldn't stay up otherwise. Getting them even was tricky; the waist slumped to one side. The trousers themselves were too long but not ridiculously so. She could roll them up and stuff them into her wellingtons if she needed to. The shirt fit better but the collar was far too big. Still, with her own blue jumper it felt like, even if it didn't look quite like, a real uniform. The blazer was too big on her shoulders. But if you weren't looking closely… she would look like Tommy. The best thing to do, she thought, was to get Michael's old winter mackintosh out of the cupboard under the stairs and wear that over the top.

It was Saturday. Her plan was to creep downstairs and march to the airfield. If she wanted to know what had happened to the plane, she would have to see for herself. They must have taken it there. She just had to sneak out of the house.

'Billie! Time to wake up!' Mrs Swift called from downstairs.

Billie hurriedly changed back into her usual clothes. She leapt down the stairs to the kitchen.

Her mother was in the corner by the fireplace. She was crouched with her back to Billie, her legs splayed and arms wide, like a goalie at a football match. She was slowly moving in on Mountbatten, a black hen, who was eyeing her with equal concentration. The feathers scattered over the kitchen tiles told Billie that this battle hadn't been an easy one.

'Open the door and I'll shepherd her out,' Mrs Swift said slowly, not taking her eyes from the bird.

'How did she get in?' Billie asked, running over to unlatch the back door.

'Your father left the door open when he went out.'

Billie opened the door, and her mother made a lunge for Mountbatten. But the hen was too fast, dodging around the woman's ankles and heading for the hallway.

'No, you don't!'

By the time Billie and her mother had caught Mountbatten (by chasing her into the sitting room and popping the waste paper bin over her head) the other chickens, on seeing the open back door, had also snuck into the kitchen.

Far from an adventure sneaking into the airfield, Billie spent the morning helping her mum clean chicken poo from the kitchen floor.

'I've decided that you should go and help the other children with the allotments next Saturday.'

Billie grunted. Those children were all younger than she was. Children her age were supposed to be looking after the pigs if they were boys, or volunteering at the British restaurant if they were girls. Billie had been dismissed from the restaurant in the summer because she ignored the customers' orders and told the kitchen what she thought best. Billie had thought this was a nice gesture but apparently not everyone wanted fish paste sandwiches.

The idea of digging allotments with little children didn't sound like fun but it wasn't as though home was any better. There was always work that needed doing. In the afternoon she helped mend the run for the chickens in the garden. She also fed Susan some bacon rind she had pocketed at tea before locking her in the coop.

Sunday brought its own delays and distractions. Church of course, and then helping her mother with the Monday wash. The Monday wash now happened on a Sunday because her mother's shifts with the ambulance meant working on Mondays. Without any home help, the wash had become one of many laundry-based Sunday jobs, along with replacing missing buttons and patching and darning things with holes in them.

By three o'clock the family had settled in the living room, listening to the afternoon play on the Home Service. Billie looked forward to listening to the children's programme at five twenty. Before then she had to sit through a boring man talking about God and then, what most confused Billie, a man's voice would start talking in Welsh. Billie knew it was the news because of the way the man spoke, like he was reading a boring shopping list. Not speaking Welsh, Billie didn't know what was being said apart from words like 'Africa' and 'Stalingrad' and 'Americans'. From the sombre way the radio announcer said these words, Billie guessed that the fighting wasn't going well.

Billie had been told, back when she was ten years old, that once the Americans joined the war it would be as good as over. The Americans had declared war in December 1941. That was nearly a year ago and all that had changed was that they had started rationing biscuits. Billie didn't consider this progress. The bombings might be less frequent, but her brother was still gone, and she still had to go to a school that didn't teach her anything.

The thought of going back to school after bunking off on Friday afternoon didn't worry Billie. She doubted she had been missed, such was Mr Hart's relaxed attitude to register taking. He probably wouldn't even notice if she didn't turn up tomorrow.

CHAPTER SIX

Both Billie's parents left early on Monday. Instructions of chores were duly forgotten and, once they'd gone, she dashed back upstairs to don her 'cadet' costume.

The driving October rain was a huge help. The large mackintosh she unearthed from the cupboard under the stairs covered much of her strange attire, and became so wet that she looked remarkably similar to everyone else on their way to work.

Billie wasn't sure of the best way into the airfield. What surprised her was how busy it was. Usually the village was sleepy with people walking into work or bicycling in. Only occasionally would you get a truck or cars. The amount of traffic this morning concerned her. Some of the trucks were RAF. In the back, uniformed figures peered down at her as she marched along the road. Cars spluttered past with rather sinister passengers in trilby hats staring out at her.

She knew what she wanted to do once inside the airfield. First, she would head for the hangars, to see if she could find the remains of the Spitfire, and from there work out what had happened to the pilot. The influx of people who all seemed to be following the same plan was unnerving. She hadn't seen the road this busy in months. She worried that there would be a queue.

Billie didn't have an umbrella and was getting thoroughly drenched. She was dry underneath her coat and, mercifully, her boots kept her feet dry but her head and hands were sodden. Water dripped off Tommy's blue cap onto her face and down the back of her neck where it was soaked up by her shirt collar. She shivered as she marched onward. A passing van sloshed the contents of a muddy puddle all over her. The spray peppered her face as well as the mackintosh. A bit of mud wouldn't stop her. In her mind she rehearsed the persona of a young cadet who, like Tommy, had loads of experience with planes and flying.

She just needed to think up a masculine-sounding name.

A few more cars passed. Some turned into the side entrance to the airfield. It was hard to see exactly where they were headed because of the rain. She could make out people walking in under large umbrellas, and even a few bicycles. Billie held her breath and carried on. She was surprised that no one seemed to be guarding this entrance. She was even more surprised when a couple of men speaking a foreign language jumped out of a truck and walked in ahead of her. If they were letting real spies in so easily, this should be a doddle.

She marched confidently past a couple of men who weren't in uniform. They were paying their taxi fare and trying to keep their camera equipment out of the rain.

'Wait you there! Boy!' one of them bellowed at her.

Billie stopped and faced them.

'Can you show us where they want us?' said the older man, as water dripped off his nose. 'Point us in the right direction? Or anywhere that's dry.'

Billie hadn't a clue what they were talking about but agreed to show them in. The fact she hadn't been this far inside the airfield since the air shows they had held before the war didn't seem to matter. She thought she'd take them with her to the hangars.

Some WAAFs looked at her in a bemused fashion from under their umbrella.

'This way gentlemen,' Billie said loudly as she marched past.

The women continued to look at Billie suspiciously but they were evidently too busy to stop her.

In the distance Billie could see a row of oddly placed aircraft. It was as though they were lined up on a mantelpiece. Or like soldiers waiting inspection. Very odd. Billie worried that the planes had been put out on display like this for a reason. Could it be for a funeral? Could the pilot she didn't even try to save be… could it be *his* funeral?

They drew near to the first of the hangars. Seeing the open entrance, she left the journalists she was escorting behind her and broke out into a run. They trotted behind, lugging their equipment. Once inside, Billie jumped up and down to get the worst of the rain off and wrang out Tommy's cap.

There didn't seem to be any sign of a broken Spitfire. On the wall was a huge sign saying, 'Remember, a concealed mistake may cost a pilot's life.' A few ground mechanics in the hangar were busy with a large piece of material. Billie assumed it to be a parachute of some sort, but it was coloured and looked heavy. Billie immediately recognised the three large twin-engined aircraft as Blenheims. Two engineers fussed over the middle plane, pointing at the blades on the propellers that weren't in line with the ones on the other side.

'Morning chaps!' A man who looked rather wetter than any man Billie had ever seen before, ran up to the two men she'd escorted. 'We've set it all up to be in front of that ship.'

A water drop dripped from his nose and landed near Billie's foot.

'You set up the cameras already? Won't they be inspecting the troops first?'

'Troops?'

The man flapped his wrists, 'Pilots, ground-crew… whatever you call them.'

'The First Lady and Mrs Churchill are going to walk and talk to some of the women pilots. I hope they bring a brolly.'

Billie put Tommy's cap back on. 'Did you say the First Lady?'

The journalists were busy attempting to light cigarettes.

'And Mrs Churchill,' the wet man nodded, failing to strike a flame.

'What? The *very* first lady?' Billie couldn't believe what she was hearing.

'That's right,' mumbled the man as he gave up on his wet lighter. 'Top brass. So, best behaviour.'

'Are you sure?' Billie said dumbfounded.

'Of course. We'd better get on. Good morning,' he said. They all shuffled towards the bomber, which was now covered with a large American flag.

Billie stood there nonplussed. It made no sense. These men were insane. The first lady couldn't be alive. And if she were, why would she be visiting a silly old airfield outside of Maidenhead in the dreariest part of England? How old must she be? Billie knew people in the Bible lived a long time, but this was ridiculous! If Eve were still alive then she would be very old indeed...

CHAPTER SEVEN

'Oi!' A familiar yelp called across the hangar. Billie turned to see Tommy running towards her. 'That's my cap!'

Just as he reached her, a woman in a sparkling wet overcoat with neat light brown hair marched up to them.

'Thomas! And,' she paused and looked tight-lipped at Billie, 'whoever you are. You are needed in the main building. Gribble has a job for you.'

'Yes Commander!' Tommy saluted, using the broom he was clutching like a rifle.

The woman sighed and rolled her eyes. 'How many times, Thomas? It's Miss Gower.'

'Yes, Miss Gower.' Tommy continued his salute until she had walked away before turning to Billie. 'Where have you come from?'

Billie dismissed his question with her own. 'Are they telling the truth? The first lady... she's coming here?'

Tommy looked at her like she was daft and pointed at the American flag draped on the bomber. 'What do you think?'

Billie couldn't work out what he meant. Was the first woman an American?

There were dozens of people moving about now. Lots of uniforms and polished boots. Tommy and Billie pushed past the press, who were setting up their cameras and headed to the main building.

Billie had assumed air bases or government offices would have access to paint or building supplies that were off limits to the rest of the world. She was wrong. The main building was a simple two-storey concrete affair, with little decoration and large windows that faced the airfield and which rattled whenever a fast train on the nearby railway line sped past. Because the windows faced the airfield, the corridor which ran along the back of the building was rather cold and narrow. It smelt of stale tea, leather sofas, pencil sharpenings and ashtrays.

They were led past doors with labels like 'Meteorological office' and 'Operations' and 'Records'.

They stopped by some pigeon holes outside a door which said, 'Pilots' briefing room'.

Before they had a chance to knock on the door, a snappish man with neat brown hair in a side parting opened it.

'Pauline found you? Good. It's under the table,' he said curtly.

Inside the smoke-filled room was an enormous antique table. Surrounding it were dozens of mismatched armchairs, ashtrays and side tables. On top of the table were two men in blue pilots' uniforms swinging their legs over the edge, talking in Polish.

'These two need that rug,' Gribble said, pointing at the tatty Persian rug under the table.

After a bit of toing and froing and bumping it into the armchairs and knocking several ashtrays over, it was decided the best course of action was for the men to lift the table and Billie and Tommy to quickly slip the rug out from under it. This wasn't done in one burst like a magician's trick with a tablecloth, but rather in several awkward heaves.

There was a commotion outside.

'Sounds like they've arrived,' Gribble said. 'Tommy, roll this monster up and take it to the hangar. The news crew need it on the stage.'

The three men fled the room, leaving Billie and Tommy to roll up the rug as best they could.

'It's so heavy!' Billie said, trying to pick up one end.

'If we tie it up to stop it unrolling, we can put it on our shoulders.'

'I'm not as strong as you!'

'Stop complaining. You're the tallest girl I've ever seen.'

It was true. Tommy heaved one end of the rug onto Billie's shoulder and then picked up the other end and placed it on his. It definitely tilted towards him. Billie staggered and wobbled as they managed to manhandle it out of the pilots' briefing room and down the corridor. The further they went, the more the rug sagged between them and the more it seemed about to unravel. Billie worried that once they left the building the rain would soak in and make it even heavier. Her neck hurt. Her head was cocked to the side by the weight of the carpet. Once at the front doors, however, a man took pity on them.

'You can't go that way, you twits!' He stood above them in the rain and grabbed hold of the rug. 'You'll spoil the pictures.'

'Sorry Mister Ralph. We need to get this to the hangar. It's for the stage,' panted Tommy.

'Heave ho!' Ralph plucked up the rug off their shoulders like it was tissue and popped it on his. 'We'll sneak round the back.'

Despite making the rug seem light, their new helper began panting too. Billie trotted after him, past lines of people in uniform, all with their backs to them, water trickling off their caps and down their necks. Billie could hear a car running and doors being opened. Evidently the guests had arrived. She could see a large black umbrella in the distance and some camera flashes.

They were off the beaten path now. Round the back of the hangars the ground was wet and spongy, and covered in thick grass. Tommy ran ahead and bashed his fist on a small doorway at the back of the hangar

'Just open it, boy!' yelled Ralph, whose temper was getting shorter the longer he stood in the rain. Billie thought she would help by holding up one end of the rug with her hands… thinking she could stay out of the rain by being under it. Her upturned sleeves were slowly filling with rainwater.

'I can't.' Tommy banged on the door. 'It's locked.'

He then yelled 'Oi!' repeatedly while drumming on the door.

The person who eventually opened the door was the last thing Billie expected to see. A small, dark woman with sharp eyes. She looked glamorous from the chin up but underneath she wore the same overalls as Ralph.

'Chile!' he exclaimed in delight. Billie thought he said 'chilly' and privately agreed with him, it was cold. 'You sweetheart!'

'I ain't your bleedin' sweetheart,' said Chile in a thick accent. She smiled at Tommy and Billie, '¡Con rapidez! ¡Niños, entren rápido! Chop, chop.'

Billie dashed inside. It was dark in the back of the hangar and the rain drummed gently on the high metal roof.

'Out the way,' Ralph said, moving past Billie as she stared up at a bomber. Before today, she'd previously only seen a Blenheim zooming overhead or as an illustration in her identification books. Billie walked under the wing. It was so much larger close up. From the ground she'd assumed that its tyres were the same size as car tyres but they were bigger than a truck's. Billie could easily duck underneath the belly of the aircraft. She gently touched its cold flank with her hand. She had an urge to rest her cheek against it.

A crowd had formed around the small wooden stage. It had been erected in front of the plane out of what looked like beer crates and wooden pallets.

'Where do you want this?' Ralph was barking at anyone who would listen.

A rotund man with a smart suit toddled up to him. 'Ah, is that the rug?'

'Nah guv, it's a bleedin' top hat,' said Ralph.

'Good show,' the man smiled. 'If you could place it on the stage.'

'It's a bit wet,' Ralph said.

'It will have to do. We need it to muffle the sounds of the footsteps, minimise creaking.'

The first lady must be very old, Billie thought again. Ralph dumped the sopping carpet onto the wooden crates.

'Don't just plonk it down!' scolded Chile. 'Es una bonita alfombra. Ten cuidado.'

'You're worse than my missus,' Ralph said.

'¡Inglés tonto!'

Tommy sidled up to Billie, nodding at the bomber.

'I've been in one of them,' he said proudly. 'I got to climb into the gun turret on the back and look out for enemy aircraft. We were only going up to Brize, so I didn't see none.'

'Have you ever been in a Spitfire?' Billie asked absentmindedly, still thinking of finding the crashed aircraft.

'What flown one? Are you daft? They don't let just anyone fly those,' he scoffed. 'I will go solo in a Tiger Moth, probably.'

'Those are the biplanes,' Billie said.

'I know what they are.' Tommy looked cross. 'What I don't know is, why aren't you at school?'

Billie thought better than to ask directly about the Spitfire she had seen crash. Its remains must be in a different hangar.

'I wanted to see her, of course,' she said pointing out of the hangar into the rain. 'Eve.'

'Who's Eve?' Tommy looked confused.

'The first lady,' Billie said.

'I thought she was called Eleanor,' Tommy muttered but Billie had already wandered over to the Blenheim. From under the wing, they watched the men hoist the second film camera high on a plinth while others set up three teetering microphones on the soggy, uneven rug.

Billie spotted Miss Gower trotting into the hangar in a large navy mackintosh, buckled at the waist. Her cap was absolutely wet through, as was her hair beneath it. But her smile and poise didn't show it. Billie thought she saw her teeth chattering as she made to walk past them.

'Ah Tommy! Well done with the carpet.' She looked sharply at Billie. 'Don't you have a cap or anything?'

Billie shook her head. Miss Gower sighed before grabbing Billie by the arm and placing her right under the American flag that was draped over the left engine.

'There,' she said, tugging the flag. 'That falls right over your forehead. Don't move from this spot while the cameras are on, understand?'

'Yes sir, commander… Miss Gower,' Billie stuttered.

'Very good.' Miss Gower marched off, still dripping, and took her place looking at the stage.

CHAPTER EIGHT

More and more women dressed like Miss Gower walked into the hangar. All were soaked. They took their places near her, with the ground crew and other men in pilots' uniforms clustered higgledy piggledy around the stage and the plane. Everyone was shuffling, trying to stay warm.

More people joined them, as the guests of honour finally made it to the platform. They were two older women, both younger-looking than Billie was expecting. As they entered the hangar everyone began clapping. Tommy nudged Billie and pointed up. Ralph was waving at them from between the plane's propellers. He had clambered up onto the wing of the plane to get a better view.

'This way, ma'am.' A man with thick round glasses holding a large black umbrella led the women to the stage.

The clicking cameras sounded like the rain as they got closer. Billie forgot her promise to Miss Gower and kept moving her head to see between the shoulders of the crowd in front of her. She wondered which of the two was the first lady. The smaller one looked sour and wore a strange fur coat but was certainly handsome. Her white hair peeked out from a neat turban. She certainly was the more put together of the two. She was nimble and elegant and the opposite of her companion.

The other woman wore a long coat and a fur stole that came down to her knees. Billie had only seen stoles like that at the cinema. They were properly luxurious. But that was about the only thing that signalled that she was in any way refined. Her hat looked, to Billie's eyes, completely out of fashion. Certainly nothing like the ones in her mother's magazines. Billie reasoned it was because she must not want to look any taller. It was flat on her head, more of a disk really. Yet she towered over most of the men even before she got to the stage. She wasn't wearing much of a heel either. She was enormous.

Unlike the smaller woman, the tall lady's face was round and wrinkled and plain. But, as she climbed onto the stage and waved at the crowd, it broke into a smile. The grinning uneven teeth and sparkling eyes made Billie forget for a second how cold she was. She suddenly thought how much she wanted to be friends with this gentle giant. Was she the first woman? She didn't look old enough, but then, to be alive now, after thousands of years... she had to have some sort of magic.

The giant turned and spoke into the cameras while the other woman sat neatly behind her on a chair placed on the stage.

'I'm very grateful for the welcome you've extended and very grateful for the opportunity to learn, which is the point of my coming to this country.'

'She sounds English,' Tommy whispered in Billie's ear.

'Shouldn't she?'

'Course not, she's American.'

Something started to tickle in the back of Billie's mind. How could the first lady be American? Surely she should be from the Middle East somewhere.

'... I apologise to all of you whom I made stand in the rain. It must have been a disagreeable experience but having lived here a long while (I spent three years at school in England) I know it is not an unusual one.'

Everyone chuckled.

'There you go, she went to school here,' Tommy said, 'that explains why she sounds proper.'

'There were schools back then?' Billie whispered back, 'Who were her teachers? Dinosaurs?'

Tommy laughed.

Tommy's reaction confirmed Billie's suspicion that it must be the smaller of the two women who was the first lady. The one who wasn't American. Although Billie still wasn't sure. After the speech was over and the rotund man had nodded to the cameras to stop filming, people started bustling around.

Ralph descended from the wing above them, jumping down without warning.

'We best get the carpet back before those BBC boys trample mud onto it.'

When they approached the stage, the large woman was still standing on it. She chatted excitedly to the gaffers as they dismantled the microphones.

Her smaller companion was complaining as she got down from the stage. 'Typical American, wasting time with the hoi polloi!'

She caught Billie looking at her and snapped her mouth shut and gave the same cold smile she'd given the cameras.

'Hello,' said Billie.

This was something Billie knew to never do. Speaking uninvited to a stranger. It was rude. It was wrong. However, what she said next was worse.

'My name's Billie. How old are you?'

The woman's eyes grew wide and her lips tightened. She marched down the steps and away from Billie. This left the tall man holding the large black umbrella in somewhat of a pickle. He was caught between the two women, one still onstage, the other marching off. He quickly chose to follow the one striding away, calling after her, 'Mrs Churchill, Mrs Churchill!'

'What happened?' Miss Gower ran up to Billie. 'Did you say anything to her?'

'Oh my,' the giant on the stage turned around to see her entourage chasing after the disgruntled Mrs Churchill. 'I suspect this is my doing; we are rather behind schedule. Poor Mrs Churchill must be awfully annoyed with me.'

'It was my fault, not yours,' Billie said.

'Shhh!' Miss Gower snapped but it was too late.

The tall lady descended the steps and made towards Billie. 'What ever did you say to her?'

Billie stared back into the shining blue eyes. 'I thought she was the first lady so I asked her how old she was.'

The tall lady let out a little chuckle. 'No wonder she sped off! Age isn't a laughing matter when you are as old as we are. You thought she was the first lady and not me?'

Billie nodded, 'I thought you couldn't be, because you're American, ma'am.'

Miss Gower and the lady exchanged confused glances.

'It may surprise you to learn that I am the First Lady and I am also American,' she said kindly. 'Does that clear it up for you?'

Bill's eyes grew big. She didn't want to accuse the woman of lying, but shook her head. 'Pardon me, but you can't be the first lady. You don't look old enough.'

'Why, what have you heard?'

'Well,' Billie shuffled awkwardly. It was obvious to Billie what the problem was, why was everyone acting so strange? 'You see ma'am, the first ever lady was called Eve and she lived thousands of years ago.'

At this, the giant figure of Eleanor Roosevelt howled with laughter. 'Oh, that's brilliant!'

Miss Gower also let out a snort of laughter. Billie couldn't work out why what she had said was so funny but all the adults seemed to have lost their minds.

'Ah, I didn't know you had such comic pilots, Pauline!' She seemed delighted by Billie and Tommy, who had stood to attention next to her.

'No,' Miss Gower said. 'I was barely aware we had any.'

'What's your name?' Eleanor loomed over Billie, who wasn't used to feeling small.

'Billie Swift, ma'am,' Billie said, relieved that she wasn't in trouble.

'How old are you, Billie?'

'She's fourteen,' Tommy said quickly before Billie could tell the truth. 'We leave school at fourteen in England. We're cadets, ma'am.'

'Have you, what's the phrase, "flown solo" yet Billie?'

Billie looked into her eyes and beamed. 'Not yet, no. Ma'am.'

'Be sure you do as soon as possible. How long does it take to train a pilot for the ATA?'

Pauline stuttered, 'That rather depends on the pilot's experience… but if they have basic competency and knowledge, they can be flying solo in a couple of months.'

'Do young ones train faster?'

'Jackie, sorry, Miss Sorour, is always going on about how she got her license at fifteen. She now delivers heavy twin-engined aircraft all over the country.'

'When is your birthday?'

Billie blinked. 'The seventh of January, ma'am.'

'I expect a letter just after Christmas then, telling me that you're a third officer.' Her eyes twinkled. 'See if you can beat Jackie's record. Now, I better break camp or we will be late to meet the women truck drivers. It was lovely to meet you both, Billie and…'

'Thomas,' Miss Gower said sharply.

'Congratulations Miss Gower. I am so impressed with everything you're doing for the war effort, for women and the young people.'

'Thank you, ma'am.'

'Thomas, Billie, you both have made my day. "The first lady". Ha! Wait until I tell Franklin. Brilliant.'

She walked away to join her entourage.

CHAPTER NINE

Billie was still buzzing from the kind things the giant woman had said to her. Pauline Gower had explained to her that the President of the United States' wife's title was the First Lady, which Billie thought was stupid.

Putting the rug back under the large table in the pilots' briefing room was much harder than taking it out. Mostly because the room was now full of impatient pilots, all with their own ideas of how to get it all the way under the table, and who had to lift what where.

Billie had the words of the First Lady floating around her head as she looked closely at the people in the room. They all wore dark blue single-breasted uniforms with distinctive buttons and pilots' 'wings' in gold, which sprouted from a circle within which the letters ATA were prominent. Some of the women had already changed out of their formal skirts and wore similar trousers to the men. Some put their damp forage caps on the radiators under the window sills, an act of habit rather than practicality as the heating wasn't on.

It was beastly cold and, as the rain eased off, the wind picked up. Billie pressed her nose to the large cold windows and made the flapping windsocks become invisible behind her breath on the glass.

'Here.' A cup was being offered by a young woman with an American drawl. 'Hot brown water.'

Billie took the tea, and tried to mimic the accent.

'Wadda,' she said.

The woman smiled at this. 'Where have you sprung from?'

'She's a spy,' said a woman with a clipped upper-class accent, dark hair and a mischievous grin. 'According to Pauline, she interrogated the First Lady.'

'Did you now?'

Billie was about to answer when a familiar whine started up. The air raid siren was much louder in the airfield buildings than it was in her house or the school. The system was supposed to come on gently, but it was so close it made Billie jump and spill tea on her trousers.

A panic wormed through her. She was a long way from the cupboard under the stairs. She watched the pilots stub out their cigarettes and murmur with irritation as they all quickly fled the room. The two women saw her dithering and waved at her to follow them. Billie tried not to think about the noise and crowds of people filling the corridor. Instead, she focused on the thing in front of her which was the black glove of the right hand of the American lady who had offered her hot brown wadda. She'd lost sight of familiar faces; Tommy had been ahead of her. By the time she got out to the front of the building she saw him and Ralph running across the airfield back towards the hangars. She hesitated; they were already so far away she wouldn't be able to catch them up.

'Come on!' the American's voice rang in her ear.

There was an air of fear. The people around them had stopped walking and had started trotting, some breaking out into a run. Billie could hear something over the drone siren and the shouting men pleading at others to hurry.

It was rare to get virtually no warning of an air raid. In White Waltham, most enemy planes flew high overhead, on their way to and from their bombing raids elsewhere. A year or so ago, Billie had been curled up under the stairs listening to hundreds of planes droning past. There hadn't been any bombs dropped until after three o'clock in the morning, when two explosions had shuddered through the house.

Her mother had been pretty shaken and had forbidden her from investigating the bomb craters. If that was how loud a bomb was from a mile away, imagine how loud they were when they landed on top of you.

The next day the radio had been full of news of how many people had died in Coventry. It was a city a long way from White Waltham. White Waltham wasn't an attractive target for the enemy, but if the Luftwaffe had bombs to spare, they would occasionally drop a couple.

Because they were far from the coast, where there were radar stations to scan the skies for incoming enemy planes, there was usually a lot of warning before the planes turned up. So most people in White Waltham didn't rush to shelter, as they never felt like there was an immediate danger. But they were in danger today.

The siren was so loud Billie couldn't hear her own feet running on the concrete path towards the bomb shelter. But, however loud the siren was, it wasn't enough to drown out the sound of what really scared her. That noise came from the spluttering gurgle of a plane, flying so low overhead she thought it was going to crash into them. What made matters more serious was the ear-cracking sound of gunfire. Was it really shooting at them? She didn't see any bullets or anyone being hit. Several of the grown-ups dived onto the wet grass.

Billie had only caught a glimpse of the plane as it passed overhead. She immediately recognised the familiar shape from her books. A Messerschmitt Bf 109. Billie hadn't fallen to the floor and followed the same American pilot as before. They reached the shelter before many of the others. The plane was still gurgling happily overhead, making another turn to come back round again. Billie heard its machine guns give a playful spurt as it turned.

The shelter looked like a grassy hill, covered in nettles and brambles. They ran down a brick-lined passage and came to a metal door on the left. It was open and a white-faced man ushered them inside.

'Move right down. Right down,' a Scottish man's voice boomed as more people came in, hot on their heels. It was calm and authoritative, as though he was bored by the idea of being peppered with bullets.

It took a moment for Billie to get used to the change in light. The shelter reminded her most of a church ceiling. It was a long concrete arch, undecorated and cold. It had a crypt-like quality to it. A prominent smell filled Billie's nose: damp soil mixed with paraffin fumes from the unlit hurricane lanterns. She followed her companion into the dark, squeezing past the men who were in the process of reaching for cigarettes or chewing gum before sitting down on a low bench against the curved walls.

'Nancy, over here!' a small South African voice squeaked.

'Jackie!' Billie's companion trotted to the far end of the shelter and squeezed in next to her.

The air raid siren faded away. Billie could still hear the engine, further away, but circling. She sat down next to the women. There were about twenty people crammed into the shelter, each sat with their back to the wall on the school benches that made up the only furniture. It was a bit bleak for a shelter. Most places kitted theirs out nicely, Billie thought.

'A morning raid!' Jackie whispered. 'It's really strange. Do you think the plane is lost?'

'He's got moxie if he is,' Nancy replied.

'Who the bloody hell told them?' The Scottish man slammed the door behind him and it went incredibly dark.

'You can't trust the Americans,' said a disembodied male voice. An English one this time. 'I bet one of them was on the blower back home last night giving every detail of Mrs Roosevelt's diary. They are children when it comes to war.'

'Hey Gribble!' Nancy called out. 'Why don't you come over here and say that again.'

This got a few chuckles from the other pilots. A chuckle that stopped as the plane flew low again.

'Nancy!' an Australian lady warned, in a whisper so the men couldn't hear, 'you'll get yourself in twouble.'

'Can we please put some lights on?' begged Jackie.

A few lamps were lit and hung from hooks in the arches. It was still hard to make out people's expressions. Murmurings of conversations broke out, mainly about the lack of ack-ack fire. It was generally agreed that the home guard had been caught off guard.

Gribble was standing up with the Scottish man, at the far end of the shelter by the door. There was an odd mix of people in the shelter. Two older woman – secretaries maybe. A cluster of male pilots, some of whom looked very old indeed. Others were younger but goofy-looking with glasses and nervous smiles. The four women sitting with Billie looked to be in their early twenties. Nancy looked relaxed, almost bored. Her dark hair had come down and was touching her collar.

Jackie, the South African, looked the youngest, her little round face was vexed with worry. 'Why isn't it bombing us?'

'It'll be after something particular,' said Nancy. 'You can't fit many bombs into a single fighter.'

'Typical Nazi,' a woman with a thick Polish accent said coldly. 'They like to watch people panic.'

'You can stop your mothers' meeting, Anna!' Gribble's voice boomed from the other end of the shelter.

'We were asking about plane,' Anna called back. 'Why is it here?'

'It could be a coincidence,' Jackie said again. 'Don't look at me like that Wamsay, things do happen by chance you know!'

'Weally jammy for them,' said the woman with the Australian accent.

'I agree. To time their air raid on the morning when President Roosevelt and Winston Churchill's wives are here seems unlikely to be a coincidence. All the planes are out of the hangars like arrows pointing at where to strike,' said the Scottish man.

'The planes are inside the hangars now. Had it come an hour earlier...' Wamsay shook her head at the thought of it. 'By wights we should have lost the lot.'

'Someone tipped them off,' Gribble said.

'Steady on old man,' said one of the male pilots.

'Who knew about the visit?' Gribble asked loudly. 'We didn't know about it until Friday afternoon...'

'I didn't know who was coming until this morning,' Nancy said. 'I thought it would be some grey general. If I had known it was Mrs Roosevelt I'd've worn lipstick.'

Gribble took his pipe out of his mouth and used it to point all the way down the long narrow shelter to the girl in her brother's uniform sat at the end. 'How did she know?'

All the heads turned towards Billie.

'Who is that?'

'I'm Billie,' said Billie. It was intimidating to have a room full of grown-ups look at her.

'Where did you come from?'

'White Waltham. By the post office.'

'And you wanted to see the First Lady and Mrs Churchill up close, eh?' Gribble asked.

'Who told you they were here today?' Anna said, in an accusing voice.

Billie didn't answer. She didn't know what to say. If she denied knowing that the First Lady and Mrs Churchill were at the airfield that morning then she would have to explain why she was there. How she had seen a plane crash and instead of helping, she had run away. That was worse than lying. But if she pretended she had known about the visit, how would she explain how she'd found out?

'She was with Tommy all morning. I wouldn't be surprised if he told her.'

'Let the girl talk,' Nancy said.

Billie stayed silent. She didn't want to get Tommy in trouble. She had already taken his cap. She was a terrible friend. She hadn't even fed Susan this morning.

'Y'all think the Luftwaffe are going to employ a girl to do their yard work?'

'They're not Rosyjski,' agreed Anna.

Billie was confused. Were they accusing her of being a spy?

'I don't know any woof laugher,' Billie said quickly.

Nancy and a few of the other women stifled giggles.

'Luftwaffe,' Billie said meekly.

'No, I like it. Watch out boys, it's the woof laugher!' Wamsey announced.

There was a collective chuckle at this, but something else had distracted Billie. They were still asking her questions. She was incredibly still, her face in concentration, listening intently.

'That's a Hurricane!' Billie jumped up.

'What is?' Nancy asked

'Listen!' Billie said.

The grown-ups stopped moving. The entire bunker cocked its head to the side.

'I don't hear anything...'

'Shhh!'

'It's a Hurricane,' Billie couldn't believe they were so hard of hearing.

'Cwikey! I hear it too!' Wamsay exclaimed.

The Scottish man shook his head. 'It's the same plane as before.'

Billie looked outraged. It sounded nothing like the plane before.

'Or another German straggler,' Gribble said haughtily.

'It is a Hurricane!' Billie insisted.

Gribble glowered at her. 'Say you're wrong, and one of us goes out there to check and gets shot at?'

'I'm not wrong,' Billie insisted.

Gribble's eyes narrowed. 'You can barely hear it.'

'Haud yer wheesht. I'll check!' The Scottish man replied and walked towards the door of the shelter. He opened it.

'The all clear hasn't sounded!' Jackie squeaked.

He'd left the door ajar and the noise of an aircraft droned past.

'I agree with the kid,' Nancy said, getting up.

Wamsey followed her. 'Wait for me!'

'You can't all go!' Jackie demanded as Anna jumped up and headed with the others for the door.

Billie joined them outside just as the Hurricane swooped low and did a barrel roll over the airfield. She was right.

CHAPTER TEN

The noise of the engine overhead and the wind blowing in her ear meant it was too loud to hear what the adults were saying. The older grown-ups walked out, looking disapprovingly at the sky. The younger pilots, however, were wide-eyed and smiling. All except Jackie, who was standing in the doorway of the shelter telling everyone they should come back inside.

Billie noticed there was another man there. He had a neat waxed moustache and wore a dark blue RAF uniform. Billie counted the stripes on his sleeves. He was a wing commander. He had a large duffle bag, as though he were about to go flying, but didn't have a helmet or goggles... She watched him approach their group from the other end of the tarmac. He looked annoyed as the Hurricane continued its aerobatics.

The plane eventually came into land on the waterlogged field. It bounced a couple of times as it splashed over the grass. Billie stood next to Nancy and heard her suck her teeth in disapproval.

'Bumpy landing,' she said.

Wamsay agreed, 'Slowed down too quickly. All that showing off and then made a wookie ewwor.'

'It's easily done,' Nancy said. 'Hurricanes are usually more forgiving than that.'

'And he didn't land there,' said Billie pointing at the nice flat surfaced runway that ran outside the main building.

Anna giggled. 'Maybe he prefers mud.'

'Have you flown one? A Hurricane I mean?' Billie asked.

'Of course,' Anna smiled.

'I'm up to class fours.' A new face appeared; Billie recognised her as the plummy woman in the pilots' briefing room. She had dark brown hair and a mischievous grin.

'Oh Diana, this is Billie.'

'What is class four?' Billie asked as the plane turned and taxied towards them.

'Advanced twin,' Diana said.

'You gotta speak plainer than that,' Nancy said.

'What class do you need to fly a Hurricane?' Billie asked.

'Class two. Class one is simple single engines, like Tiger Moths and Swordfish. Class two is single-engined fighters with a bit more oomph. Class three are light twins…'

Billie interrupted, 'What is a twin? Two engines?'

Nancy smiled. 'That's it. Class threes are planes like that Anson over there. And fours are heavier aircraft, like the Blenheim.'

'Is there a class five?'

'Of course, four engines,' Diana said, as the Hurricane taxied towards them. 'Like Halifaxes and Lancasters.'

'No woman has flown solo in those yet,' Nancy said somewhat bitterly.

'Lettice is training for it,' Anna said.

'Pauline is weally working her hard. If she passes, we'll all be allowed to twain on them,' Wamsay said.

'And if she doesn't, we'll all be written off as incapable,' Diana said bitterly.

'But you all have been flying Hurricanes and Spitfires?' Billie said.

'Of course,' they all said together.

Billie didn't know how to react. She knew that women flew planes. She'd grown up knowing the names of Amelia Earhart and Amy Johnson. She even knew women flew planes at this airfield. There had been a lot of talk about women helping with the war effort. People complained they were taking jobs away from the men and that women couldn't do the same jobs as men. Billie was under the impression that the women working in the airfield flew non-war planes. There had been pictures of them in the papers in biplanes. It hadn't occurred to her that the aircraft she saw everyday were flown by women too. It seemed a bit weird, the idea that a woman could fly a fighter plane. It both upset Billie and excited her. It was like she had discovered a lie and felt stupid for believing it.

'You don't,' she hesitated, 'you don't fly them into battle or anything do you?'

'Lord no!' Diana laughed. 'We deliver them from the factories to the RAF bases.'

'And American bases,' Nancy added.

The Hurricane finally came to a stop in front of them.

'For God's sake,' shouted Gribble, 'radiator flaps! The ruddy thing will catch fire!'

'That's half a crown fine,' Diana muttered.

'I like her running a little hot.'

A smiling gentleman jumped out. He was handsome with blond hair and wore an RAF uniform under his thick flight jacket. He did a naval salute and shouted down. 'Aye, Aye, Captain Foulweather!'

'It's Fairweather, ya nincompoop,' the Scottish man hollered back.

'Bumpy landing?' asked Diana pointedly

'No,' the pilot lied, jumping down off the wing. 'I've had plenty of bumpy landings but they usually involve combat, something your pretty little head wouldn't understand.'

'Play nicely,' whispered Nancy to Diana, who had gritted her teeth in a forced smile.

'It's a surprise to see you, Stone.' Gribble stepped forward. 'I wonder if we could have a word with Wills together? We need to write a report on…'

'Sure thing, old man,' Stone said, only half-listening. 'What on earth is this? Another sprog?'

He was looking at Billie.

'Hello,' said Billie.

'Blimey, this one is barely out of nappies.' Stone spun round. 'Where is that Gower girl? She's behind this.'

'*Commander* Gower must be in a shelter somewhere,' Diana said. 'There is an air raid going on.'

Stone looked confused. 'Now?'

'Aye,' said Fairweather.

'Shouldn't we all be taking cover?'

'That's what I said,' nodded Jackie.

'We were until we heard your plane.' Nancy explained. 'Billie recognised it as a Hurricane before we even heard the engine.'

'Really?' The moustached RAF officer looked curiously at Billie.

'I thought it was still that Messerschmitt,' Gribble said.

'With ears like that she should join the Wrens. They could use her as radar!' Stone looked around expecting a laugh and when none was forthcoming, he addressed Billie directly. 'You should be called Dumbo.'

Billie was confused as to why she was being compared with a film about a baby elephant with large ears. 'Dumbo couldn't hear better than anyone else. He could fly though.'

Stone's eyes narrowed, 'I suppose that is where the two of you differ.'

'And I'm not an elephant,' agreed Billie.

Stone looked at Diana. 'Is she a bit touched, this one?'

Billie didn't understand what he meant by that but it certainly seemed to anger Nancy, who stood eye to chin with him and glared, 'I never heard such a pretty man be so ugly.'

Stone seemed to enjoy the confrontation, smiling at Nancy as she squared up to him. 'Ah, so you think I'm good-looking?'

'Stone,' the wing commander interjected, 'shall we go indoors?'

'I was hoping Wills and I could ask him a few questions first,' Gribble said but was ignored.

Stone shot Gribble a triumphant look and followed the RAF Officer back towards the main building. The all-clear siren started.

'He's not nice,' Billie said to Jackie as they followed them back to the main building.

'He's ex-RAF. He doesn't have to be nice,' Jackie said wisely. 'If I'd botched a landing like that when I shouldn't be flying anyway, I'd be reprimanded.'

'Why shouldn't he be flying?'

Jackie shrugged. 'He's in trouble with the high ups. Wills, he's the man in charge of operations, didn't want him back. Stone's got Wing Commander Cummings in his pocket, though. That's who came out to meet him.'

Billie hung back, looking to see if she could see Tommy among the men coming out of a shelter by the hangars.

'Has Pauline told you what you are doing?' Nancy asked her.

Billie paused. The right thing to do would be to go straight home, get changed and apologise to Mr Hart for bunking off. But she still was none the wiser about the Spitfire crash or if the pilot had survived.

'Because if she hasn't,' Nancy said, 'I'm down to be a taxi pilot today. I'll be flying everyone in the Anson.' Nancy said pointing at the twin-engined plane. 'There'll be a spare seat up front.'

CHAPTER ELEVEN

'Y'all hurry up. Or we'll hit bad weather,' Nancy shouted.

Billie was sitting in a plane. A real plane. She had never been in a plane. She felt a little sick. Her heart was pounding. It was happening. What was more exciting than being in a plane was being in a cockpit. It reminded her most of a tiny greenhouse only instead of pots and mud and plants in front of her were two steering columns, a couple of levers and a range of gauges. It didn't smell of a greenhouse either. Her nose was filled with a mix of engine oil and aviation fuel. And kippers, someone must have eaten them today. Nancy was sat to the left of her, a small book on her lap.

Billie kept looking out of the window. Her palms were sweaty as she clung to the thick strap that pinned her tightly into her seat. The whole plane wobbled as pilots clambered through the tiny door on the wing and sat in the seats behind. The last person on was the Scottish pilot called Fairweather.

'What are you reading?' Billie asked.

'The pilots' notes,' Nancy said, 'the gyro is U/S but other than that, she looks in good shape.'

'U/S?'

'It means it is unserviceable and doesn't work.'

Billie wondered what a gyro did but kept her worry to herself. She also worried that Nancy would think she knew anything about how planes worked. She only knew what was in her reference books. She watched Tommy and Ralph step out from under one of the wings.

'What are they doing?'

'Just making sure the flaps are all secure, and there's no damage to the aircraft,' Jackie said.

'Damage?' Billie echoed in a worried voice.

'She's an old girl but she's as reliable as they come,' Diana said cheerily. 'You read the snag about her left wing? Slight dent. I imagine it will increase the stalling speed a little.'

Billie wondered for a moment what a stalling speed meant. She'd travelled in a car when it had stalled at a junction. It had given this great lurch and the engine had cut out. Not a big deal on the tarmac, she thought. But to stall in the air... that sounded terrifying.

'Noted. OK. Clear!' Nancy yelled.

Nancy turned over the engines, a strange 'pew, pew, pew' noise made Billie's head whip round. The propellers began to turn and Nancy quickly flicked a switch above them and the engines spluttered and started to purr. It was incredibly loud.

The plane bumped along the grass towards the surfaced runway. Everything seemed to be rattling.

'H for hydraulics, T for trimmers,' Nancy said loudly over the noise of the propellers. She was checking various switches and gauges. 'T for throttle.'

'I thought you said T for trimmers?' Billie shouted over the propellers.

'The first T is for trimmers, the second is to check the throttle friction.' Jackie said in her ear.

Billie looked nervously back at the other pilots sitting in the rows of seats behind the cockpit. They all looked reassuringly bored.

'On take-off, the throttle can move back,' Diana explained as Billie twisted round in her seat to hear her. 'It happened to me coming out of Thorney Island. I was in a Hampden, and when I took off, the acceleration pushed me back so far in my seat I couldn't reach the throttle...'

'Americans make planes for giants,' confirmed Jackie.

'Why didn't you ask for a cushion?' Wamsay asked

'They didn't have one! I'd put my parachute behind me so I could reach the pedals... but had nothing behind my shoulders. That Hampden had a kick like a Thunderbolt. So when I took off my back was pinned against the seat and I couldn't reach the throttle levers.'

Nancy continued her checks. 'M for mixture, rich... P for pitch. P for petrol we've plenty of that... F for flaps... they're moving your side too, Billie?'

Billie looked out the window and saw bits of the wing wiggling up and down. She nodded.

Diana was busy adding drama to her near death take-off. 'I was bent backwards. And that's when I saw the right-hand throttle lever started to slip back, because the tension nuts were loose. The whole plane began to swing to the right as the right-hand motor was losing power. And I was spiralling into the hangar...'

'G for gills, temperature, carb, heat and icers...' Nancy continued.

'I managed to wriggle into a ball and bring my right leg up and kicked the throttle forward. The engine roared back to full power, and I saw the runway windsock veer past, just inches beneath me,' Diana said proudly.

'Thank goodness you are flexible.'

'Hurry up Nancy,' Wamsay said. 'Annie Anson won't give us no dwama.'

'She's setting a good example,' Fairweather said. 'Leave her be.'

'Don't listen to Foulweather. I want to be back before tomorrow,' said Anna in her thick Polish accent.

'Doors locked?' Nancy called back to the passengers.

'Probably,' they replied.

Billie held onto her seat belt more tightly.

'Giddy up!' said Nancy.

The propellers, which had been chugging happily away, changed note. It was like being trapped in a jam jar with giant bees. Billie held her breath. The plane sped forwards. She was expecting it to shoot right up into the air so was confused when it felt like they were tipping forwards as the rear wheel left the ground. Then they hung for a second, before slowly rising, like they were driving up a gentle slope.

Billie watched mesmerised as the trees slid beneath them. She felt elated, relieved and then without warning, the plane dropped.

Billie felt herself fall like she'd come off a swing. She nearly cried out. But as soon as disaster struck it disappeared. The plane swooped back up, banging Billie hard in the elbow as she reached out to hang onto something.

Several people swore. Nancy breathed out a long slow stream of air as she steadied her nerves.

'Wake turbulence!' shouted Diana.

'I see the laddie.' Fairweather tapped on the window. 'Looks like a Halifax.'

'It must be going some lick to leave a wake that large.'

'Everyone ok?' Nancy asked.

They all murmured assent.

'Let's get out of these hot pockets,' Nancy said and turned the plane.

Billie eyed the ground beneath her as they swooped Westwards.

'OK Bill, now it's time for your job.'

Billie looked round. 'My job?'

'You're co-pilot,' Nancy said. 'I need you to winch up the wheels.'

Billie looked at her like she was mad. 'What? Go outside?'

Nancy laughed, 'Don't be daft. See that crank? Start turning it. It'll take you a while, but it'll give you arms like Popeye.'

Billie leant forward and began turning the handle. It was stiff. After ten turns she looked up.

'Keep on going,' Nancy grinned.

It took Billie about five minutes before the landing gear clicked into the fuselage. She was a bit sweaty. Her hand had the start of a small blister on it.

'Don't worry,' said Nancy, 'It's only this first bit that we will need the gear up on, all the rest will be much shorter legs. We'll leave it down for those.'

'We are going to several places?'

'Correct,' Nancy said happily. 'Each pilot needs dropping off at different factories and air-fields.'

'Will you be doing the evening taxi?' Jackie asked.

'I'm going to hitch a lift to Windsor if I can,' Diana said breezily. 'A group of us are going out tonight and I can get a lift into London from there.'

'Going to a nightclub on a Monday? You're crazy.'

'You only live once.'

Billie still couldn't believe she was up in the air. They were flying below the clouds. Which really wasn't very high. Churches and farms, swept beneath them. A dark brown river, orange leaves on the trees. When they neared a large town, the smoke billowed and mixed with the cloud above it, making a yellow, streaky haze. Over the buildings were the dark shadows of balloons

82

looming like teachers in an exam room. There were cars and trucks, horses and carts. Billie could just about make out people moving too, a bicycle and someone walking their dog. Nancy was following the railway line, heading north towards Oxford. Billie spotted a steam train as it chugged south towards London.

She felt so separate from it, like the real world was actually no more than the dolls' houses. How strange that it felt safer to be hundreds of feet up in the air than it did walking around with the grown-ups and their problems.

The noise of the engine was much more rhythmic inside the plane. It purred in and out, like laying your head next to a happy cat.

'Bill,' Nancy shouted, 'we need something to land on.'

She pointed at the winch. Billie bent forward, the straps pulling her back as she heard the engines change tone.

'Quick Bill, we're entering the circuit,' Nancy yelled.

Billie was relieved it was much easier lowering the landing gear than winching it up. It was disconcerting feeling the plane gently drop and turn. The engine note changed while she was bent forward.

'All done?'

'I think so?' Billie said, sitting up. She could see an airfield out of the window, the different colours of the grass indicating a landing strip. Tents were pitched close by and there were planes and jeeps over by a large hangar.

'Let's find out.'

They landed with a little bump, all three wheels making contact. Billie had lowered the landing gear correctly. They sped across the wet grass and suddenly Billie realised how grey everything was again.

Nancy encouraged Billie to stretch her legs but they weren't on the ground for long.

One after the other, each pilot was dropped at a different airfield. Nancy had a map with her, that she would consult every now and then. She pointed out strange shaped fields, roads and hills she used to navigate by.

Eventually it was just Nancy and Billie left in the plane. They didn't speak much as the noise of the engines were so loud, but they exchanged glances. Glances that made Billie feel happy. Nancy was enjoying showing her how the plane worked, taking the yoke and turning it so the plane wobbled from side to side. The yoke in front of Billie also moved at the same time, making it look like they were dancing. This made Billie giggle, partly because it was silly but mostly because it made her nervous. Like being tickled.

'Your turn!' Nancy smiled. She was pointing at the column in front of Billie.

Billie stared at her, dumbfounded.

'Don't be chicken, take the controls!'

'No!' Billie simply couldn't believe what was being asked of her.

'Take them, or...' Nancy pulled her yoke to the left, making the plane bank sharply. 'We crash!'

Billie looked flabbergasted.

'I'm not kidding,' Nancy said, 'the more I bank, the slower she will go and that means she won't be going fast enough to stay in the air. We'll drop out of the sky.'

She let it go and crossed her arms, leaving the plane to slowly spiral.

'You're crazy!' Billie yelled. It felt like they were going to flip upside down at any moment. Billie grasped the controls.

She yanked them to the right. Nancy cackled as the plane threatened to flip over in the other direction.

'Yeehaw!' Nancy whooped. She was playing with the throttle levers in front of her, and pressing the pedals to either counter or exaggerate Billie's mistakes – Billie wasn't sure which.

Billie corrected again, a little more gently this time. The plane lurched.

'Argh!' Billie shouted as the plane wobbled this way and that.

'Look at this instrument here,' Nancy said, pointing at what first looked to Billie like a compass. 'It's the artificial horizon, it's like a spirit level.'

'What's a spirit level?'

'Like a glass of water on a shelf. You can see how flat it is by looking at the water line in a glass. That's what this is. You gotta make her fly flat.'

Billie stared intently at the gauge as it swung this and that way with the plane until the plane was flying more or less level. She looked over at Nancy, who had a big grin on her face.

'Now just point the nose to wherever you want to go,' Nancy smiled.

For the briefest moment Billie had the image of crossing over the sea and rescuing her brother. How she'd break him out of prison and hug him. As she did, she moved the controls towards her... this made something in her stomach wriggle.

'We're falling!' she yelled at Nancy.

'You've put the nose in the air and that's increased drag. That's slowing us down. If you want to speed up, you need to increase the throttle,' she pointed at the little levers on the console between them.

Billie did as she was told and adjusted the levers. The engines roared. They began climbing. The clouds got closer and closer.

Billie flinched as she braced for the impact.

The plane rose into them with no change, not even a shudder. It was totally white. They were still rising. 'How do we get down again?'

'I told you, point her where you want her.'

Billie moved the nose down but didn't touch the throttle. They were back down out of the clouds, heading rather too quickly for the ground.

'If you want to go faster, we need to adjust the trim,' Nancy suggested.

'I want to go slower!' yelled Billie.

'Why didn't you say? Pull her up to level,' they slowed and the plane levelled out again.

'Want to have a go at landing her?' Nancy grinned.

'No thank you,' Billie said, her heart still pounding.

Nancy spotted White Waltham, and joined the circuit.

She began her system of checks, 'Petrol, brakes, fuel boosters on, hydraulics, undercarriage is already down, mixture, flaps, pitch, gills.'

Billie smiled and looked down at her house, the school and church as the Anson gently turned and headed for the surfaced runway. Nancy landed it perfectly.

'So, what now?' She said as they slowed down.

'Um,' Billie said trying to recall from the last time they had landed, 'tail wheel unlock. Gills open...'

'Half-a-crown fine if you forget...' prompted Nancy.

'Flaps up!' Billie remembered.

'We'll make a pilot of you yet.'

CHAPTER TWELVE

Pauline Gower was eating a sandwich in her office. She shared the space with two other individuals, as there were three desks. One had a large map across it. The other had another sandwich on a plate that Billie couldn't take her eyes off. She was so hungry.

'I don't enjoy telling young people off,' Pauline said curtly. 'I've no children and when I do have them, I hope not to have to do it too often.'

Billie tore her eyes away from the sandwich and faced the commander.

'We have procedures here. Procedures to keep you and everyone on this airfield safe. We can't do that if you don't tell us you're coming or give us details of who to contact if you were to go missing. Nancy.'

'Yes ma'am?'

'You should know better than to let someone fly without them having been cleared first.'

'I didn't know she hadn't been, ma'am. I assumed she was a young cadet.'

'Where did you pop up from?' Miss Gower looked at Billie.

'I live in White Waltham…' began Billie.

'…next to the Post Office, I heard.' Pauline gave Billie a shrewd look. 'Did you hear about the First Lady and want to see her, or do you have it in your head that you can be a fighter pilot?'

Billie knew she had to be careful with what to say next. If she pretended she had been at the airfield to see the First Lady, she could get Tommy in trouble. They would think he had been gossiping. If she said she wanted to be a fighter pilot, they would think she was delusional.

'I do like flying,' she said. 'But I don't want to be in a dog battle or anything.'

Pauline smirked despite herself. 'We have a long waiting list of brilliant women who are trying to become ATA pilots. You would be the youngest by a long way at fourteen. Do you have any experience of flying?'

Billie looked at Nancy, who eyed her as if to say, 'Don't tell her too much.'

'Yes,' Billie said.

'Pops... excuse me, Commodore d'Erlanger who started the ATA, always says to look for the ones who show spirit and initiative.'

'We call it hustle,' Nancy smiled.

Pauline raised her eyebrows. 'Yes, but Americans also refer to bottoms as fannies so let's not get carried away.'

Billie managed to contain a giggle.

Pauline pointed to a collection of letters on the desk, which were in a variety of stationery stacked in three piles by the telephone. 'So, tell me, Billie. What makes you think I should choose to train you over all of those letters from other keen young women wanting to fly?'

Billie thought for a moment. 'Because you let the First Lady think I had already started?'

Pauline opened her mouth and shut it again.

'Very well. Come in warm clothing tomorrow. We will get you started on the basics.'

***

When Billie got home, she took off her brother's suit and scrunched it in a ball under her bed. She couldn't let her mother find out she'd been in her brother's room. No one was allowed in there. Not until he came home.

She got dressed in her usual skirt and jumper and bounced downstairs. She cut herself a thick slice of the dry national loaf her mother insisted she eat. She skipped putting margarine on it but smeared it with a thin layer of her father's marmalade. Cramming it into her mouth she ran to the tap and poured herself a mug of cold water. She poured the water into her mouth at the same time as chewing the dry bread. The noise was extraordinary.

Hiccupping as water dripped onto her jumper, she looked out the window above the kitchen sink. Susan was roosting in the apple tree again. She tore a corner off her slice and took it out to her.

'How did you break out?' she asked Susan, offering the crust.

The chicken took one look at Billie and scampered away to hide in the bush by the long brick wall that ran down the side of the garden to the disused outside loo at the back.

Billie reached out to her through the twigs, trying to get the piece of bread closer. 'I'm sorry I scared you last week. I didn't know the plane would land on us.'

Susan sat, eyeing her. Just out of reach.

Billie went to turn over some of the loose bricks to see if there were any worms or fat spiders she could offer the bird. It was as she was trying to pick up a particularly slippery worm that Susan made a broody noise and jumped up on the bricks next to her.

'I didn't find anything out about the Spitfire we saw.' Billie said pensively. 'But something strange is going on. The pilots think that someone told the woof... the Luftwaffe that the First Lady was at the airfield and that is why they tried to attack it. Only they got their timing wrong and were too late.'

Susan made the noise again. A half cluck. She watched carefully to see if the other hens got too close.

'Haven't you been listening?' Billie said frustrated. 'Even the older pilots thought someone must have tipped them off. They suspected me.'

Susan picked up her head and clucked.

'Of course I'm not a spy!' Billie frowned. 'But someone might be...'

It was at this point that Billie's mother returned home. And Billie realised she hadn't peeled the potatoes. Or posted the letters her mother had given her on Friday.

'You're home early!' Billie said.

'You needn't sound pleased about it. Mrs Ganderlilly says she's going to slaughter the rabbits a week on Friday, once the babies are weaned.'

Billie didn't like the idea of rabbits for dinner. And said so. She was ignored.

'Any eggs?' her mother asked

'It's only just getting dark.' Billie said, knowing all too well that there hadn't been any laid. She placed Susan onto the ramp to the coop.

'What did you do at school today?'

'There was an air raid,' Billie said, nudging Susan into the coop with the others and shutting the door.

'In the daytime?' Billie's mother walked her into the house.

'Yes,' Billie sat down at the kitchen table. 'Do you think this means that they are going to start another invasion?'

'No, no, no, they're busy in North Africa. Hitler's attention is divided between there and Russia. I've no idea why they want to attack Russia. Sounds like a ghastly place. Can you imagine killing the royal family?'

Billie thought killing the rabbits sounded worse but didn't say so.

'Still, it might bring an end to the war.'

For Billie's mother, everything that happened in the papers might bring an end to the war. Billie often wondered if she cared who won, as long as the prisoners were allowed to return home.

'What will happen if we lose?' Billie asked.

'We're not going to lose,' her mother snapped.

'The Germans sound like they are winning in Stalingrad, it said on the radio…'

'They won't in winter.'

'But they survived last winter…'

'Look I'm not Mountbatten!' Billie's mother started and, before Billie could interrupt, she clarified, 'the general not the chicken. We need to be patient.'

Billie didn't look convinced. 'It's almost 1943 and has anything changed? It feels like we're losing.'

'That's enough! No one is losing!' Mrs Swift snapped. 'Except the Nazis. Who, if they aren't losing right now, will definitely be losing soon. Have you been at your father's marmalade?'

'When the war is over, I'm going to eat an entire pot of jam with a spoon,' Billie said firmly.

'All you think about is your stomach! Our boys are dying out there and you only care about yourself!'

Billie looked down.

'Think of all those little girls in France who have German soldiers living in their houses and brutalising their families. I think we all need to make more of a sacrifice.'

Billie looked worried.

'Yes,' Billie's mother said. 'We waste too much. If the birds are too old to produce eggs, then we can make do with them another way. Starting with Susan.'

Billie looked horrified. 'No, Mummy!'

'We could have a proper meal on Sunday and I could use the bones to make a decent stock that I could take to the canteen on Monday.'

Billie started to cry. 'No! She's having a bad week!'

'She better have a better week! It is high time you realise just how serious this war is, and how much other people suffer for your benefit. Susan's lived long enough. It's her time.'

Billie felt the world slip away from under her, just like when she had taken off that afternoon. She didn't remember how she had got upstairs, whether her mother had led her, or just shouted at her, or she had run up there herself. Either way, she put her head under the pillow and screamed tears of despair into the cold fabric. Not Susan. Not her best friend.

CHAPTER THIRTEEN

The prospect of losing Susan had put all other thoughts out of Billie's mind. Her mother left early the next morning. Billie sat in the drizzle, watching the chickens eat their grain. There were only two eggs in the coop. Two eggs from seven chickens, and no way to prove Susan had laid either of them. The ginger bird cocked her head at Billie, who promptly burst into tears.

She had managed to get snot on her school cardigan and was looking around for the washcloth when there was a knock at the door.

It was Nancy.

'The house next to the post office. Just as you said,' she said. 'What's eaten you?'

'M-m-y m-m-mother wants to k-kill Susan,' Billie sputtered.

'Goodness, whatever for?'

'Sunday lunch.'

'Susan is a rabbit?'

'A chicken,' Billie sobbed.

'Can't you ask her to kill a different chicken?'

'I love all of them. But Susan's one of the oldest. And she's stopped laying eggs.'

Nancy paused. 'The solution is simple enough.'

'It is?'

'Yes. If Susan can't provide your mother with eggs, then you must.'

'But I can't lay eggs,' Billie reasoned.

'No. But I bet you we can find someone who can get us some.'

'How? Eggs are rationed to one fresh egg a week!' Billie wailed.

'We'll work it out. Now, go get into something warm We'll be late.'

Billie hurried upstairs and once again raided her brother's bedroom for a pair of trousers. She wore her usual school vest and shirt and jumper over the top. She carefully shut the door again and bounded downstairs.

Nancy was chatting to the milk woman outside the house by the time Billie ran up to her.

'I miss my horse,' Nancy said, patting the mare.

'You can have this one love,' the milk woman tutted. 'I'd do a better job with a cat.'

Billie carefully put the bottle of milk in the coolest part of the parlour before running out to find Nancy again, this time further up the road.

According to Nancy they were late. It was five minutes past eight by the time they arrived at the main building. Nancy moved quickly through the corridor, replying to the 'good mornings' with a 'hey' or a 'howdy'.

They made quick progress between each room. First, she picked up her 'chit' from her pigeon hole. Billie followed her like a duckling to the 'met office', then to 'maps and signals' where Nancy bent low over the desk, carefully marking on her precious map the new position of the barrage balloons, removing the positions she'd previously noted in pencil. Nancy had a special pocket in her jacket for her rubber, which she called an eraser.

'Can't lose that,' she said patting it, 'they are rarer than bananas.'

There were people on telephones everywhere. It felt futuristic to Billie. They knew about the weather all over the country and could speak to anyone, anywhere. Billie waited patiently, watching the women and boys who weren't in uniform run in and out of the rooms, delivering notes and post to various desks and pigeon holes. Just as Nancy was about to leave, two men walked in, blocking the door. One was a man called Commander Wills; Billie knew this because Nancy squeaked it in her ear. The other Billie recognised from his moustache as Wing Commander Cummings who had saved Stone from Gribble.

'...I was hoping to break five hundred flying hours this month but nothing doing,' Wills said softly. 'I won't be back in the air 'til December now.'

'They give you chaps less time off than our boys!'

'It's not as though we are fighting,' Wills said. 'Oh, this is Nancy Bamford. She's one of the Americans that got sent over last year, before Pearl Harbour mind. Tell me, what days do you get free?'

'Usually you get one day a week for one week, then two days the next week. Weather dependent,' Nancy said.

'I can't imagine it ever raining on you,' Cummings' smile looked decidedly creepy to Billie, he turned to her. 'You're the cadet with the good ears!'

'This is Billie Swift.' Nancy smiled, gesturing at Billie, who looked wild-eyed at the two men.

Wills nodded. 'Where did Pauline find you?'

'Next to the post office,' Billie stuttered. 'I... er... I have a hustle.'

Cummings laughed. 'You're fun. Watch out for Stone, he'll show up in your classes.'

'Nice to see you Nancy, Billie.' The two men walked past and carried on their conversation.

'Commander Wills is the senior CO of the whole of Number One Ferry Pool,' Nancy whispered. 'Dang, I wish I'd asked him to send me on better deliveries.'

They made their way to the pilots' briefing room and Billie was handed a hot tea before she had even had the opportunity to refuse one. She held it close to her, letting the steam rise up and warm her face. The Ministry of Information had decreed that heating was not allowed to be switched on until November as part of a government drive to save fuel. Billie thought the quantity of hot drinks being made likely offset the supposed savings.

'We dwink hot orange squash at Hamble,' Wamsay said. 'It's wevolting.'

Billie was surprised to see Chile in the briefing room. She had met her yesterday in the hangar and had assumed she was part of the ground crew and not a pilot. She wore a flying uniform like the others, only it had a funny flag on her shoulder.

'Fog,' said Chile. That wasn't all she said. She swore too.

Even though the weather was pretty clear in White Waltham, according to the met office there was no use flying for a few hours. The general mood in the briefing room was one of impatience.

There was a knock at the door, and a woman in a nurse's uniform not too dissimilar from Billie's mother's uniform shouted, 'Swift!'

Heads turned towards Billie.

'It must be your medical,' Nancy nudged her.

'My what?'

'Take my advice,' Diana said earnestly, 'lie down on the floor before they read your height. It will make you taller. You're supposed to be five foot five.'

'How will that work?' Lettice Curtis asked airily.

'It's air pwessure isn't it?' Wamsay jumped in. 'All that weight pressing down on you.'

'Go on,' Nancy shoved Billie towards the nurse.

Tall though she was, there was no way Billie was five foot five. She was led into a small room marked 'Medical'. In it was a doctor's desk and a bed on wheels. The nurse said, 'Keep your underwear on, otherwise pop everything on that chair.'

Billie stripped down to her vest and pants and did as Wamsay had suggested. She didn't feel much taller, but she was a lot colder by the time the doctor came in.

He was another elderly figure, with thick glasses and shaky hands.

'Can you measure me right away?' Billie asked from the floor.

This caused him to jump. 'Goodness, a flying, talking carpet.'

Billie didn't stand up until the last moment. As he lowered the ruler onto her head, she gently raised her back heels off the ground. Thanks to his shaking hands he didn't seem to notice.

She took an eye test, then he listened to her heart and looked in her ears and her throat.

'You seem healthy enough, and have an above average limb number for an ATA pilot.'

Billie recalled the older men in the pilots' briefing room. Several were missing arms and there were a few with canes too, which made her wonder if they had all their legs.

'The only thing that kills pilots is bravado,' he said sorrowfully. 'And I've no way of measuring that. Anyway, you're fit as a fiddle. My advice is to keep us informed if you are planning a family...'

Billie wondered how thick his glasses were if he hadn't realised she wasn't even an adult, let alone married.

'... only if you fly above twelve thousand feet with child, they tend to make an early appearance.'

Billie put her clothes back on and made her way back to the mess.

She'd only just managed to find a fresh cup of tea when another voice called from the door.

'Oi! Chile! Dumbo!' It was Stone. 'You're late for class.'

'Class?' Billie asked

Chile swore again. '¡Pensé que empezaba a las nueve!'

'See y'all,' Nancy waved.

Billie followed Stone into the corridor, walking into a different part of the building.

They went into a room Billie hadn't visited before. Inside was Gribble looking cross and Tommy sitting happily at one of the desks. It was a proper classroom and with only five people inside it, a lot calmer and nicer than Billie's classroom at school.

'Good morning,' Gribble said gruffly.

'Morning,' Stone said, equally coolly. He evidently didn't want to be there.

Tommy had an exercise book open with the day's date written in the corner.

'Books and pencils are over there.'

Stone picked one up, walked all the way to the back of the room, slumped down at a desk and put his feet on a chair.

Billie grabbed a pencil and sat down next to Tommy. Chile sat behind them.

'Isn't this good?' Tommy whispered. 'We're being given proper flight lessons.'

'I'm your instructor, William Gribble,' said Gribble.

'We know who you are,' drawled Stone.

'I teach class threes and above, but Wills has given me a special assignment,' Gribble said with an air of resentment. 'It appears some of our pilots don't follow the rules. While others haven't mastered English. So, we are going to do a crash course.'

'Stone is already good at crash,' Chile said.

'¿Qué?' said Stone.

Gribble pretended not to hear them. 'We will go over it all, as fast as possible. You can get flight observation hours by accompanying the taxi. And mechanical instruction by working with the ground technicians. We will do our flight tests in January. Until I pass you, you are all grounded until the New Year.'

'What? That's two months!' Stone spat.

'This course is a reminder,' Gribble carried on, 'of both the principles of manned flight but also of how

ATA pilots are expected to behave. To this end, and because we can't send those under sixteen to learn at Thame, Commander Gower thought it a good idea to have our youngest cadets join in to give them a head start and make sure we properly cover all the basics.'

Billie and Tommy looked at each other excitedly.

The lesson was much better than school. Billie had to draw a plane in her book and show how the air moving above the wing took longer, and how this meant it was under less pressure and that's what caused it to lift. She also learnt that stalling an aeroplane was not like stalling a car. You could stall a plane with the engines running and you could still land a plane with no engines at all. If there wasn't enough air flowing over the wing the plane would lose height until the point where there was not enough to keep it up at all. Then it would simply drop out of the air.

Billie couldn't be happier.

CHAPTER FOURTEEN

Billie returned home to find Susan hadn't laid an egg but had managed to get out of the pen. She was rooting round the vegetable patch. Maybe Billie's mother would spare her if she knew Susan was a slug destroyer?

Billie was now on her best behaviour. Everything was neat and tidy. She didn't eat any of the apricot jam. She didn't ask for the radio to be turned on. She didn't dare mention Susan at all. Perhaps her mother would forget.

It wasn't until eight in the evening when her mother checked the pantry that she asked after the eggs.

'Two,' Billie admitted.

'Two eggs! There should be at least five. They're not moulting so it isn't that.'

'It's the cold snap,' Billie said. 'I'll clean out the coop tomorrow morning and stuff it with the fresh hay.'

'I see what you're trying to do. But she's an old bird. And the others don't like her.'

'So what, if the others don't like her?' Billie said. '*I* like her.'

'Chickens can tell when a chicken is bad. That's why they peck at her.'

'They do not!'

'We can't afford to spend our egg ration on chicken feed if those chickens refuse to lay eggs.' Mrs Swift looked down at her daughter with folded arms. 'Susan is for the chop.'

'But you don't know who it is who is laying!' Billie said. 'It's not fair, she could be the only one laying and if you murder her, we'll have no eggs at all.'

***

Following Gribble's lessons was hard work. He delighted in long-winded, complicated explanations and never repeated himself. Billie was getting better at taking notes, though she still spent some time copying Chile. What was strange to Billie though was how much Stone resented the lessons. He deliberately tried to anger Gribble, offering stupid answers.

'Right,' Gribble said, addressing Chile, 'what happens if you suffer engine failure?'

'I look for a place to force land,' Chile said coolly.

'Before then.'

'If engine is no working, I keep trying restart her. If still no working I, ¿qué es la palabra?... I feather her.'

'Good. Tommy, what is feathering?'

'Um...' Tommy frowned.

Stone swore. 'Can we just move on?'

'It is where you stop the propeller moving isn't it?' Tommy said. 'Lock it in place.'

'How should they be positioned? Billie?'

Billie frowned. 'Does it matter? I mean you just want them to stop spinning...'

'Why should the propeller blades be rotated parallel to the airflow in the case of engine failure?'

Everyone was quiet.

'Stone?'

'This is stupid.'

'You want to reduce the drag as much as possible because she will go faster for longer and this give you more time before she stall,' Chile said.

'Exactly.'

'Can we just get into a plane, do a few circuits? Any decent pilot knows, flying a plane is an art not a science.'

Gribble smoothed his hair in an exasperated way. 'As you well know, Stone, in a plane crash you only have seconds to act. The longer you can stay in the air, the more time you have to look for alternatives and the greater your chance of survival.'

'Oh yeah, and how many crashes have you been in?' Stone asked.

'I've had to make a forced landing before now.'

'One?' Stone scoffed, 'I've had loads.'

'Does crashing a lot make you a better pilot?' Billie asked.

Even Gribble laughed. Stone looked furious. Billie did her best to avoid him when they stopped for lunch.

'Pie and beans please,' Tommy said to the lady behind the counter.

'Tommy?' Billie said, looking at the menu in the mess. 'Can I borrow some money?'

'That means I can't get pudding!'

'They've only got stewed fruit.'

'With custard!' he said mournfully, handing over a sixpence. 'You can pay me back when you get your pay packet.'

Billie looked surprised. 'I get paid?'

'Not much but it pays for the lessons and a bit extra. You'll get less than me because you're a girl.' He frowned. 'You better be paid less than me.'

'Thank you. Pie please.'

'Shall we sit by the window? At least away from Stone,' Tommy said.

Billie sat down with her meal, took a forkful of hot pie and sighed happily. 'I like learning about flight.'

'It suits you.' Tommy said.

'How do you mean?

'You're usually grey and insipid-looking, but when you're calculating airspeed, I dunno, you look pretty.'

Billie was taken aback. 'You think I'm pretty?'

'No,' he said firmly. 'I'm just saying you look less… lost? This morning you looked like you'd been crying.'

Billie had been crying. She suddenly remembered Susan, and her mother's threat to eat her if she didn't lay any eggs. She gasped and looked at Tommy urgently. 'Do you have any eggs?'

'In my pie?'

'No, any eggs. I need eggs for the weekend. I can give them back after. It's a matter of life and death.' Billie hesitated. 'I need them for my hen.'

Tommy was frozen with his fork halfway to his mouth. 'No, I was wrong, you're not pretty at all.'

'You're mean!' Billie said.

'I bought you lunch!' He sighed. 'Don't you have any spare eggs? Like in water-glass or anything?'

Billie thought back to the time she had helped her father prepare the large earthenware jar of water-glass. They had followed the instructions on a government pamphlet but either the powder had been faulty or an egg had cracked at the bottom. By the time they had tested it, all the eggs had gone off. She shook her head.

'They've probably got a few jars here,' Tommy pointed towards the kitchen door.

'You think I should steal them?'

Tommy looked shocked. 'No! I thought you could ask.'

Billie felt immediately stupid. Why did her brain jump to stealing? She was a bad person. Tommy could see it. She wanted to run away.

But Tommy didn't notice how red in the face Billie had become. 'If you are going to ask, the chicken coops are round the side of the main building. Ralph takes care of them. As long as he gets 'em back I don't see the harm.'

That might just work. If she could borrow the eggs, then pop them into the chicken coop every morning... she could return them once her mother had seen them. It would look like Susan was laying, and she wouldn't be killed.

CHAPTER FIFTEEN

Billie wasn't far from the chicken coops when she rounded the corner and saw Stone. He was writing a note on his knee. Funny place to write a note, when there were warm desks indoors. She eyed him as she strode past but he wasn't in the mood to let her leave.

'Dumbo,' Stone jumped up and grabbed her by the arm. 'I've got my eye on you.'

'Just one?' Billie asked.

'You're the reason why everyone was out on the runway to see me do that bumpy landing on Monday.'

'I only said I heard a Hurricane.'

'Why do you have it in for me, Dumbo? Why do you try and show me up in front of Gribble?' His eyes narrowed. 'What have you heard about me?'

'Nothing,' said Billie.

He kept staring at her, his hand still clasped around her arm. She wondered what he was about to do. In a film, the actress would cry out or burst into tears. Maybe he was trying to kiss her. They did that in films too. The look of revulsion on his face told Billie this probably wasn't what he was doing. He seemed to be waiting for her to say something.

If there was one thing that Billie was good at, it was not saying anything. She was happy to leave conversations at 'hello'. Stone was under the impression that most people will talk if you let silence hang. Billie thought that saying nothing was the best way to avoid saying the wrong thing.

'You just stay out of my way,' Stone said eventually.

That was going to be tricky to do, Billie thought.

'No,' she said.

His moustache twitched. He let her go and stormed away.

Billie found the chicken coops. Sure enough, Ralph was there.

'We've had problems introducing some of the younger ones. Had to put a new roost in,' Ralph explained.

'Could I borrow some eggs? Mine aren't laying at the moment.'

'Have you thought about why yours have stopped laying?'

Billie thought of the Spitfire and scrabbling to get Susan out of the brambles.

'I think something spooked them. Mountbatten broke into the kitchen at the weekend. Mum chased her with a saucepan. That might have done it.'

'You named your hen Mountbatten?'

'I had to,' Billie said. 'We only had two to start, Susan and Alexander. Mrs Ganderlilly thought Alexander was a cockerel. Mum got three others and my brother named them all after famous commanders. And when he left, we got Mountbatten and Harris. I just kept the tradition going.'

'But you didn't rename Susan?'

'She won't respond to anything else,' Billie said. 'Anyway, I'm sure they'll lay again soon. If I could borrow the eggs, I'll bring them back on Monday.'

'The kitchen needs these ones, but I can get you half a dozen on Saturday. Be careful, mind. If they aren't back by Monday, you'll be hearing from me.'

'Thank you.'

'Now, in return you're going to do me a favour.'

What Ralph wanted was simple. To get a message to Nancy telling her that she wasn't going to be able to get to London that evening because he had yet to find a replacement tyre for Diana's car.

'The one I was promised turned out to be for a truck.'

Nancy was going to have to make her own way to London, which would be easier for her if she didn't fly back to White Waltham first. The only problem was that Ralph didn't know where she was to get the message to her.

The location of aircraft factories and air bases were top secret, as the Nazis could target them for bombing. The only people who knew where Nancy was worked in a room called 'Operations'. And the door was always locked, even when people were inside.

Billie had been in there with Nancy on her first day to pick up their chits. She knocked on the large wooden door.

'Hello, what's this?' A tall man she'd never seen before, with slicked hair and wire glasses, looked down at her.

'I'm Bill,' said Billie before looking at his uniform and adding, 'sir'.

'Right,' said the man at the door.

'Who are you, officer?' asked Billie, surprised that he hadn't reciprocated her greeting.

'I'm Death,' he said.

'Hello Death,' Billie said brightly. 'I was hoping to ask Commander Wills a question. Is he here?'

'Yes…' Death said, his eyes narrowing. 'I'm afraid he's on the telephone at the moment.'

'I need to know where Nancy Bamford is.'

'Why?'

'Because Ralph in ground crew bought a truck tyre by accident.'

'And…'

'If she wants a lift tonight, she can't get one.'

'And you want to bother Commander Wills with this vital information?'

'No,' Billie said, 'but he's the only person I know who works in here, and I need to get a message to her.'

At this point Commander Wills walked out of the door, chewing on the end of his unlit pipe.

'Afternoon, Commander,' Billie chirruped.

'Afternoon, Billie,' he muttered back.

Death looked suspiciously at Billie. 'You can go in, but be quick. Ask Sally. She'll sort you out.'

He slid through the doorway and followed Commander Wills, walking up the corridor.

CHAPTER SIXTEEN

Inside it was obvious who Sally was. She was the only woman.

'Hello,' she said, still typing on her typewriter. 'Can I help?'

'I need to work out where Nancy is and get a message to her.'

Sally nodded at the chalkboard on the wall. 'Her position should be up to date on that board.'

Billie ran over to it. It had the pilots, class, leave, their position and their last signal written in columns... H. Ellis... K. Jopp... N. Bamford. The position however was written in a code Billie didn't understand.

'What does FP15 mean?' she asked as Sally continued to type.

'That's Hamble,' Sally said.

'She has left there and is taking a Spitfire to?'

'Stoney Cross.'

'And then she took a Tomahawk from there to Cosford, FP12... then, is due to be picked up by another taxi pilot there.'

'Seems right,' Sally said, still typing as Billie stood looking at the chalkboard.

'Is there any way I can send her a message so she knows she can't get a lift tonight?'

'She can't?'

'No, Ralph couldn't get a wheel for Diana's car.'

Sally stopped typing. 'He told you this?'

'He told me the wheel he got was for a truck.'

'But he didn't tell me this?'

Billie thought for a moment. 'Did he not?'

'No! I was supposed to be getting a lift in Diana's car too.' She stopped typing. 'Unbelievable!'

'Can we get a message to her?'

'You can use the phone,' She sniffed. 'Not that it will be much good. Cosford is miles away; she won't be able to hitch a lift from there. We'll be having another boring night in, away from the city lights. What beastly news.'

Billie went to the phone. Someone had helpfully taped a note to it that said 'dial 00 for operator' on the handle. It made a crackling 'burrr' sound when she held the receiver to her ear. She put her finger in the hole and whizzed the dial all the way around, enjoying the 'tring' as it travelled back.

'Number please,' said the operator.

'Hello I need Cosford Airfield please, the ATA.'

'Do you have a number please?'

Billie saw a notepad with all the ferry pool numbers and their four-digit phone numbers next to them. 'Yes, Cosford 1694.'

She waited a moment and there was a chatter in the background from the other end of other women saying 'Number please. Putting you through now.' Billie wondered what their offices looked like. They sounded like they were underwater which made Billie think of a bathroom. She imagined them as mermaids, with clips on their nose and a big tangle of wires that they had to find the ends of, all numbered with tags. She listened intently to see if she could make out any splashing.

'Putting you through now.'

Billie expected to hear a click and a hum and the ringing of a telephone waiting to be picked up at the other airfield. What she actually got was a click and a crackle and then a man's voice.

'...I don't see how we can get away with it. They aren't even letting me fly Tiger Moths at the moment...'

The voice was familiar. It whispered, as if scared of being overheard.

'No, not next week. Unless you arrange it. Getting a plane will be tricky, I've been put back in Kindergarten. It's made our whole operation much harder...'

It was Stone. She could only hear his side of the conversation... and what he was saying was decidedly strange.

'That's great. If I can get those you-know-what's to you once I'm cleared to fly...'

There was a pause as presumably the man Stone was talking to was responding. Billie wanted to know what a 'you-know-what' was.

'No, no, no... If they catch wind of this... it will be more than my pilot's licence on the line.'

Billie wondered what was could be worse than losing your pilot's licence... Did he mean he was going to commit a crime?

'They not picking up?' asked Sally.

'What was that? This line is terrible.' Stone could hear them.

Billie put her finger to her lips and keenly listened.

'No, alright. I'll make the drop. Friday thirteenth? I hope you're not superstitious.'

A drop? Did that mean Stone was going to deliver something to someone? There was nothing of value at White Waltham other than the planes themselves. Then again, Billie was surrounded by sheets detailing plane deliveries and top secret RAF strategies as well as maps and weather data. But who would want that? The enemy?

Billie shuddered.

'What's the matter?' Sally asked.

He had gone. Billie put down the phone.

'Crossed line,' said Billie.

Sally raised her eyebrows. 'And you were eavesdropping?'

Billie nodded.

'That's bad manners! Get off that phone. *I'll* call Cosford.'

'But on the line there was…'

'I don't want to know. It is rude to listen in on private conversations.'

'But…'

She picked up the phone and pointed at the door as a signal for Billie to get out. 'And you can tell Ralph he's a cad.'

Billie certainly wasn't going to do that.

CHAPTER SEVENTEEN

Billie spent the morning with Nancy, who was on taxi plane duty. This time, however, she had VIP guests. Wing Commander Cummings was delivered to an airfield in Kent. He had been effusive, congratulating Nancy on a 'daisy cutter of a landing' and saying the Americans were mad not to have her fly for them.

'I can get my paws on some home comforts,' he said, clutching his hat over his heart. 'I'm working with the Americans. They have all sort of candies and things.'

'And what would you want in return?' Nancy said coolly.

'It would be an excuse to see you again,' Cummings said, smoothing his moustache.

'We see each other plenty,' Nancy said. 'You're always at White Waltham.'

'I have to keep Stone in check,' he winked. 'At least until he gets clearance to return to the squadron.'

'He's not too old?' Nancy asked.

'He's only twenty-six,' Cummings said. 'I best be off. Are you sure I can't get you…?'

'No, thank you, Wingco,' Nancy smiled.

Billie frowned, watching the little man walk across the airfield. 'You were saying how much you missed coffee and peanut butter.'

'So?'

'He said he could get you some.'

'But to do that what rules would he be breaking?'

'Who cares?' Billie said.

'Men die every day trying to cross the Atlantic with supplies from America,' Nancy said seriously. 'I won't have them risk their lives just to let a man like Cummings believe he's in with a chance with me.'

'But the supplies are already here…'

'And who is to say how Cummings will get hold of them? I bet he'll ask a colonel he's pals with. They'll take the supplies from their men's rations. It would be unfair.'

Billie felt a bit resentful towards Nancy. She wanted to ask Cummings for some American aircraft magazines.

From Kent they had taken some stuffy RAF officers and some scruffy mail sacks to an airfield near London.

It was nerve-racking as a passenger, watching Nancy negotiate the barrage balloons that protected the buildings and factories below. Each enormous balloon was tethered to the ground by a line. Billie knew that if the wind blew in their direction or if the plane clipped a line, that would be the end for all of them. Fortunately, Nancy kept a level head and stuck to her flightpath.

They returned to White Waltham. Nancy had a lot of paperwork to do before she could join Billie in the briefing room.

Stone was sitting in one of the leather armchairs opposite another pilot who wore an eyepatch and had only one arm. Billie recognised the older man as Jopp. Neither paid each other any attention but when Billie entered Stone's eyes narrowed. 'This is a pilot's briefing room. Are you an officer?'

'Nancy told me to wait here for her.'

'Well, you must do what Nancy says,' he said with an air of snark. He rose up out of his chair and strode over and leant on the large table, staring at her. 'What are you wearing?'

Billie blushed a little, 'it's my brother's old suit.'

Stone scoffed. 'Personally, I don't think women should wear trousers. It isn't exactly fetching.'

Billie wondered why she would need to be fetching. 'I think Nancy and Diana look nice in their trousers.'

'Diana would look nice in a dishcloth. How come your brother leant you his suit?'

Billie looked down at her feet. 'He didn't. I borrowed it.'

'You can't borrow something without them lending it to you. That's stealing!'

Bill's bottom lip began to tremble. 'I couldn't ask him.'

'Why not?'

'He's...' She held her breath for a moment and said, 'he's a POW.'

Stone sucked his teeth, 'Yeah, that's a tough one. I bet you'd rather he was dead than not knowing if he'll ever come home.'

Billie blinked. 'No, I don't want him to die!'

Stone shrugged. 'I'd rather die than be a prisoner of the Nazis. It nearly happened to me once.'

There was a disgruntled cough and shuffle from Jopp.

'Yeah,' said Stone looking up, jutting his chin out. 'This was 1940. Crazy time. That's when it was just us in the war. France had surrendered, and the Nazi forces were set on invasion. The only thing stopping them was me. And the rest of the RAF. I had been chasing this Jerry in my Hurricane. I prefer them to Spits, more grunt, you know?'

'No,' said Billie.

'I'd intercepted him over Kent. Got a hit and the scallywag bolted back to the sea. It doesn't count as a kill unless you down them, and my tally wasn't as impressive as it is now. So, I chased him over the water. By the time I shot him down I was damn near France, but I was so intent on the kill I hadn't checked my fuel. Maybe I caught a stray bullet in the old fuel tank…'

'Wouldn't that make the plane explode?'

Stone didn't like being interrupted. '… So I ran out of juice. Had to do a forced landing on occupied territory. I risked getting captured on land rather than drowning in a choppy ocean. They saw me go down, and I had to kill a couple of 'em with my pocket knife while I hid. Eventually I got in touch with the resistance who smuggled me back home. It took four days. But yeah, I'd've rather died than get caught.'

'Is that why you're with the ATA now and not the RAF? Because you crashed a plane?'

There was a laugh that quickly transformed into a cough from the armchair.

'I haven't left the air force,' Stone spat. 'I'm waiting to go back, but the paperwork is taking longer than expected.'

'Is that why you're in the wrong uniform?'

'No point in getting a new uniform when I will be back dogfighting with the Jerries in a few weeks.' He sniffed. 'Until then I'm stuck with the old farts and idiot schoolgirls.'

'But you get to fly,' Billie said. 'Once Gribble clears you. And flying is fun.'

He scoffed. 'This isn't flying.'

Billie looked confused. 'No, we are in a building.'

'You really are stupid,' he said. 'Ferrying broken planes to factories and new planes to air bases, isn't real flying.'

'But you're in a plane, and you're flying.'

'Flying is doing barrel rolls, diving, shooting the enemy, sinking battleships and escaping in and out of the clouds!' He smoothed his hair back and jutted his chin.

'You did a barrel roll on Monday in the Hurricane.'

'Yes, and I got in trouble for it,' he said bitterly. 'The stupid rules they have here. No acrobatics, no flying after dark or above the clouds, no flying close to barrage balloons, no radio, no flying with instruments. That last one is stupid. If they taught people how to fly with instruments, then they could fly above the clouds!

And I am an RAF fighter pilot, I know how to fly a damn plane.'

'But you crashed,' Billie said.

'That was a life-or-death situation,' Stone snapped.

'And the crash last week?' Nancy was stood in the doorway, with her parachute hoisted under her arm.

'What about it?' Stone said.

'Downing a Spitfire in a field less than a mile from the airfield. Was that a life-or-death situation?'

Stone got up off the table and stood menacingly. 'That wasn't my fault.'

Billie couldn't believe her luck. Was it Stone who she had seen crash? He had survived it! She needn't have worried that she hadn't helped! She hadn't killed anyone. The pilot was very much alive and decidedly unpleasant.

'What are you grinning at?'

'I'm happy you crashed the plane,' Billie said.

He looked furious. 'That. Wasn't. My. Fault.'

'We don't know that do we?' Nancy said, taking off her flying jacket to put a jumper on. 'Because you refuse to help the investigation.'

'There was nothing to investigate!' He spat. 'The ruddy thing set itself on fire. They only want to do an investigation to try and get me in trouble.'

'They want an investigation to work out what happened,' Nancy said. 'It's not about blame.'

'Of course it is!' he shouted. 'Your tiny woman brain can't possibly see what's going on. D'Erlanger wants me here, but that man Foulweather and Professor Grumble want me out. They're jealous of me. I'm young, I'm fit, and I'm a real war hero. They are looking for any excuse to boot me and if they do that, the RAF won't have me back.'

Nancy sighed. 'Remember when I crashed that Tiger Moth because I got confused about which runway we were using and taxied straight into Anna's Mosquito? That accident was all my fault, and they still let me fly. The investigation process isn't about blame.'

'You're as daft as Dumbo,' he said, pointing at Billie. 'Why would they do an investigation if it isn't to pass the blame onto me?'

'To work out what happened,' Nancy said calmly. 'So they can stop it from happening again to someone else who might not be so lucky... or so skilled as to force land a plane while it was on fire... even if it did land upside down.'

He was about to interrupt her again but shut his mouth when she called him skilled. Instead, he huffed. 'They can do their stupid investigation without me.'

He walked away from them and made for the door.

'But they can't do it properly if you don't help them.'

'I'm not writing my own termination letter. You daft Yank.'

Billie's head was filled with questions. The Spitfire she saw crash hadn't been on fire. It hadn't had its engines on at all and there had been no smoke. But it had crashed less than a mile away from the airfield and it had tipped up and landed upside down. Were they talking about the same plane? Why had Stone let Nancy believe the Spitfire had been on fire?

CHAPTER EIGHTEEN

Billie was relieved when she checked the coop that evening that the hens had laid two eggs.

'String-bean, I'm sorry,' her mother said when Billie came in with the eggs in a bowl and Susan cradled in her arms. 'Two chickens out of seven are laying eggs. That's less than the summer.'

Billie did a quick calculation. 'If they laid three eggs, would you reconsider?'

'Why are you so fond of that hen? Other little girls make friends and talk about boys and horses and dancing and things.'

'Other girls don't like me,' Billie said.

'You don't give them a chance to like you!'

'Chickens like me.'

Bill's mother pursed her lips. It was true. She could never hold Susan like Billie could.

'Don't you want to be normal? You don't even read proper books. That copy of *Black Beauty* is collecting dust in your room. You can't enjoy reading those tedious catalogues.'

Billie felt a little frustrated. The knowledge she had gained from reading her reference books meant she could excel at the airfield. But she couldn't tell her mother that she hadn't been in school all week.

Bill's mother continued, 'You were too close to your brother. It's my fault, I should have pushed you into more social activities sooner.'

Billie stroked Susan on her lap.

'Saturday!' Billie's mother exclaimed. 'Did you put your name down for the allotment volunteers like I asked?'

Billie knew she was expected to work at the airfield on Saturday. 'I could volunteer at the airfield at the weekends.'

'No darling,' she shook her head. 'That's dangerous. And not ladylike.'

'They have women there,' Billie tried a different tack. 'And chickens.'

'What would you be doing?'

'Oh,' Billie said, 'delivering chits and messages, sorting the post and washing and repairing the planes.'

'No, I refuse you to have anything to do with heavy machinery. You'll get your fingers nipped off or your leg wound round a propeller.'

It was clear that Mrs Swift imagined a hangar to be like some Victorian cotton mill.

'I don't think that's likely.'

'And what if a plane crashes on top of you?' She shook her head 'What is wrong with volunteering on the allotments?'

'Some of the kids from school are collecting rag and scrap for the war effort.'

'I know, they come round after church on Sundays.'

'They are organising a big drive in Maidenhead,' Billie lied. She studied her mother's expression. It was disgust so she quickly added. 'They are also doing a raffle that was a huge success in Henley.'

Mentioning Henley was a dirty trick. It played into her mother's snobbery. Henley was by far the most well-to-do village in the area, that is if you didn't count the great stately home of Cliveden which was almost as grand as Windsor Castle, which itself was only a few miles away.

'Oh? What are they raising money for? More planes?'

'Probably,' said Billie, remembering the money raising drives from years ago.

'That sounds less dangerous than mechanics,' Mrs Swift said, dumping vegetables into a pot and placing them on the stove.

'Can I go then?'

'As long as you're keeping out of trouble and doing something for the war effort.'

***

Billie certainly was doing something for the war effort. She was trying to catch a spy. Getting evidence was a lot trickier than Billie had first thought. It was made harder by all the small jobs and deliveries that anyone passing her seemed to offload on her.

'Take this to there.' 'Give so-and-so this message.' 'Can you get everyone tea?'

Stone meanwhile sat quietly in the back of Gribble's classes.

They were learning about meteorology, and how to plan an optimum flight path.

'When you go to maps and signals, you mark on your map all the balloons and ack-ack positions so that if you do find you have to alter your course you know where to avoid...'

'Are we going to maps and signals at any point?' Stone asked. 'Only, in case you weren't aware, my map was taken off me.'

'It wasn't taken, it was put there with the others in the cupboard for safekeeping. Since you're grounded…'

'Why am I grounded? Almost everyone in the ATA has made a forced landing and I'm the only one that's punished?'

'Here we go again,' Chile said.

'The pride of the ATA, as well as our can-do spirit, is the value we place on mutual learning and on accident investigation.' Gribble was trying to keep his temper. 'There are things which don't add up about your accident and you refuse to tell us what happened.'

'Because you are trying to persecute me!' Stone shouted and stormed out the room.

'He acts like a twelve-year-old!' Gribble said, watching the door slam shut.

Billie felt a bit put out by that.

'Dumbo… sorry, Billie can you tell him that we are going to go out to the hangars in an hour and he can find us there if he wants to re-join.'

Billie got up from her desk and went to find Stone. She guessed he'd be in the briefing room or maybe the mess, trying to wrangle a free sausage from the cooks.

Instead, she found him outside ops… listening at the door.

'What do you want?' he snorted, standing up.

'What are you doing?' Billie asked. Though it was obvious what he was doing. Why he was spying on ops worried her. Was losing his temper in class just an act so he could get away and spy? Who was he spying for?

'Mind your business,' he glared at her, daring her to question him.

'Gribble says that we're heading out to the hangars in an hour and you can meet us there after you've calmed down.'

He looked furious. 'I AM CALM!'

'Why not just tell them what happened?' Billie asked.

'I did, but they want to go over it again and again,' he growled. 'It's like they think I'm lying.'

'But you *are* lying,' Billie said coolly.

'I am NOT.'

'You said the engine was on fire which is why you made a forced landing, but the engine wasn't on,' Billie said, remembering what she and Susan had witnessed on the hill. 'And I'm pretty sure the propeller wasn't feathered.'

His jaw hung open. 'Who told you that?'

'No one,' Billie said.

'Was it Cummings?'

'No one needed to tell me, I saw it all. I was there.'

'You… you saw me set fire to it?'

Billie didn't correct him. He looked young for a moment and like he was going to be sick. He took a deep breath.

'Have you told anyone?'

Billie shook her head. 'No. But you should.'

Stone had crashed and set fire to a Spitfire, then lied about what had happened. What had happened? Why would he do that? Maybe there was something on the plane that he didn't want discovered. Secret plans or messages from the enemy?

A tingle of worry entered Billie's head as she remembered Stone's angry face telling her to keep out of his way. If he really was a traitor, if he was fighting for the other side, and he knew that she suspected him... would that not put her life in danger?

CHAPTER NINETEEN

Bill's arms and hands were covered in black muck after helping Ralph fix a leak in the hydraulics of a Westerland Lysander. Billie liked the Lysander, which had odd-shaped high wings that reminded her of a dragonfly. It was a friendly looking aircraft with big chunky 'boots'.

She then had to clean out a Spitfire. Inside the cockpit she'd discovered an empty French cigarette packet along with a farthing and a sewing kit.

She, of course, pocketed the lot. Nancy would have taken it to show everyone, thrown away the cigarette packet and given the farthing to charity.

At the end of the day, she followed Ralph to the hen coop where, as promised, he gave her a box of six eggs in a paper bag. She thanked him and stayed to watch the chickens while he went to deal with a Swordfish that was having problems on the runway.

Billie looked at the large chicken run in front of her. She wanted to go into the run, carefully peak inside the coops and pocket any extra eggs that were in there. Ralph had only given her six, which still might not be enough to convince her mother that the chickens were laying normally.

Before Susan saw the accident, they had usually laid four or five eggs a day between the seven of them. This number had reduced to none or two. Susan was stressed and her strange behaviour was affecting the others.

All the ATA hens were inside sheltering from the fine drizzle. All she needed to do was unlatch the gate, walk in and lift up the coop lid. She could just do it to see, just to look…

She found herself doing exactly that. When she looked inside a few chickens bolted from the nest box, clucking loudly. She felt a mixture of disappointment and relief when she saw the nest was empty. If there was an egg there, she felt sure she would have stolen it.

'Pinching eggs?' The sudden bark of a man's voice caused Billie to drop the lid of the next box with a bang.

'No!' she squeaked. 'I was just looking.'

It was Stone. 'What do you want eggs for?'

'I don't want eggs,' she lied. 'I wanted to see if there were any.'

'Why?'

'My chickens haven't been laying,' Billie said. 'I want to see if these ones are having problems too.'

'You need eggs?' he asked casually. 'I could get you eggs.'

Billie looked at him curiously. 'Why would you get me eggs? You don't like me.'

'Listen Dumbo, it's not that I don't like you…'

'But you don't,' Billie said, while a random hen clucked approval.

'Shut up!' He ran his hands through his hair. 'Why do you have to make everything so difficult?'

'Why don't grown-ups ever say what they mean? They talk and talk and make less sense than a chicken.'

'Why are you so stupid?' he shouted.

'Why are you so mean?' she shouted back.

'I'm trying to be nice! You're like one of those giant machines in Master of the World. Or the tin man.' He began to sing, 'Just because I'm presumin' that she could be kind-a-human, if she only had a heart.'

'Leave me alone.'

'You don't get to tell me what to do!' he snapped. 'And if you tell anyone, ANYONE what you think you might have seen…'

'About you crashing the Spitfire?'

'Shhh! If you tell anyone I will tell them I caught you stealing eggs.'

'I haven't stolen any eggs.'

'Oh yeah what's in that bag?'

'Nothing!' Billie said clutching the bag closer to her.

'Who is anyone going to believe, an RAF pilot who fought in the Battle of Britain or a mechanical child whose only friends are idiot chickens?'

He had a point, thought Billie.

CHAPTER TWENTY

When she was home Billie checked for eggs. There was only one. She sighed and carefully placed the borrowed eggs alongside it.

She let Susan into the kitchen and she began peeling the potatoes, carefully placing each peeling into the bucket for the pig slop man. Susan wasn't exactly helping, trying to balance on the edge of the bucket so it fell over. Eventually she settled on Billie's socks. Her claws were scratchy at first but once she puffed her feathers up, Billie's feet were soon the warmest part of her body.

'Evening,' Billie's mother said as she bustled in from work. 'String-bean, that hen needs to be with the others in the coop.'

Billie sighed. 'I thought keeping her warm might help her lay more eggs. And then you would decide not to murder her.'

'Don't be so dramatic.' Her mother went over to the sink as if to start washing her hands. 'I had to help Dr Bundock change a tyre. I'm not sure how I'll get to work tomorrow. Walk, no doubt. Did you check the eggs?'

'No,' Billie lied.

'I'll do that before I get my fingers wet.'

Billie smiled to herself.

'Your little hen appears to be on our side after all,' Billie's mother barrelled through the door. 'Seven eggs! Incredible.'

'It is the weather,' Billie said. 'They need more heat. I told you more hay would do it.'

'As long as they don't get mites,' her mother said. 'Which means regular cleaning out.'

'So,' Billie said, watching her mother eye up the eggs, 'Susan is safe?'

Her mother rolled her eyes. 'Yes darling, but you shouldn't get so attached to mindless creatures. You should try and make real friends.'

Susan clucked.

The good news about Susan's reprieve didn't last long. On Sunday, instead of her father's usual breakfast of toast and jam, he was given a slice of bacon and a mound of scrambled eggs.

'It's an omelette,' Billie's mother said proudly. 'It's not powdered eggs, we had so many I thought you could have a treat. Fresh eggs. And we got some cream. Plus, there is rabbit pie for lunch. It has been a very good week.'

Billie watched as her father tucked into the eggs and winced. She had been a fool to think her mother wouldn't use the eggs. Now she had to get half a dozen eggs to replace the ones she'd borrowed from Ralph. This was more complicated than she'd thought.

***

First thing on Monday, Billie bumped into Ralph outside the wooden hut beside the hangars.

'Did you have Sunday off?' he asked.

Billie nodded. 'Cadets get every Sunday off and every other Saturday.'

'Thursdays are my leave day at the moment. Not very Christian making me work on Sunday. Talking of, I wasn't being Christian lending you those eggs.'

'What?' Billie was confused.

'Neither a borrower nor a lender be,' quoted Ralph. 'It's in the Bible.'

'That's not the Bible,' Billie said.

Ralph cocked his head in the way Susan did when she was locked in the run. 'Isn't it?'

'It's Hamlet,' Billie said. 'William Shakespeare.'

'Bleedin' heck, I thought you had a gift for planes. I didn't know you were a veritable poet an' all.'

Billie looked confused, it seemed obvious to her that anyone who knew planes would know Shakespeare. 'The complete works of Shakespeare are on the same shelf as *Aircraft of the World* and *Aircraft Recognition*. So I read it after I'd finished those.'

'Why?'

'I like to do things in order.'

'Why are the books next to each other? They're different subjects.'

'Eric Sargent is next to R.A. Saville-Sneath and next is William Shakespeare. I thought you were supposed to order books by the author's last name. Is that not right?'

Ralph blinked. 'Fair enough. Anyway, do you have 'em?'

'The books?'

'The eggs!'

'Not right now…'

'Make sure you do, or I will have to charge you interest. And my demands will be eggstortionate! Get it?' he laughed.

'No,' said Billie.

'Well make sure you have 'em next time I see yer.'

'Alright.' Billie agreed, trying to keep the worry out of her voice.

Avoiding Ralph was hard to do. Particularly when she and Tommy were supposed to be helping him in the mornings while Gribble taught Lettice and the male pilots how to fly class five aircraft.

Instead, she joined Nancy in the Anson, taking the pilots to the various airbases and factories. Nancy would often let her take control after take-off, and she learnt the cheats of how to map-read whilst flying, and practising sharp turns and manoeuvres while maintaining airspeed so they wouldn't stall.

'You're doing great in a twin. You'll be fine in a single engine. It's much easier – only one throttle,' Nancy said as they taxied towards the hangars at White Waltham.

'Hey,' Tommy greeted them when they got out. 'Ralph said he'll be in first thing tomorrow in the far hangar and you can meet him there.'

Billie nodded. But she didn't go and see Ralph the next day. She couldn't face him until she had saved up enough eggs to pay him back. The trouble was, the hens were only laying one or two a day and she couldn't take those as she didn't want her mother thinking they weren't laying any. Not when Susan was already being a nuisance by pooing on the rug in the living room after escaping the coop. Billie tried to explain to Susan that she had to take it easy.

'Harris is eating more than you,' Billie told her. 'You need to peck her head more. Tell her who's boss. I don't like the bread I have to eat. Or the cabbage. But Mum makes me clean my plate every time and you need to eat your feed.'

Susan cocked her head to the side and walked somewhat defiantly past Billie and slipped out of the gate.

Billie swore. 'Fine. Get your head chopped off. See if I care!'

But she did care.

CHAPTER TWENTY-ONE

It wasn't just Billie who was avoiding part of her crash flying course. Stone was absent for some of the instruction. He was also acting strangely. He hadn't stopped calling Billie 'Dumbo' but he seemed to be paying more attention to Gribble in class.

'You'll all be even more pleased,' said Gribble, handing each of them a piece of paper, 'that we are going to do a test.'

Billie scowled. She was never good at tests; she didn't see the point in answering questions she didn't care about. She knew that Henry VIII had six wives but why did she have to write it down? It didn't make any sense to her. She only wanted to 'do well' when she understood the exact reward and even then she would only do well on tests she actually had an interest in.

'Draw and label all the different parts of a single engine fighter plane. From memory. Chile, this is just as much about spelling and English as it is about technical knowledge.'

Chile nodded. Stone remained silent.

'Now,' continued Gribble. 'Whoever gets most right will win a prize. Your very own pigeon hole in the briefing room.'

'Chile and I already have our own pigeon holes,' Stone muttered.

'It's a bit of fun,' Gribble said, handing him a pencil.

Both Tommy and Billie's eyes widened at the prospect of a pigeon hole. This was not only a sign they were on their way to becoming real pilots but it also meant they could receive post. Without anyone else knowing. Billie could order a magazine and have it delivered to her pigeon hole without her parents' knowledge.

Billie immediately drew the outline of a Spitfire and began labelling everything as quickly as possible. Her eyes slid over to see what Tommy was drawing. His plane didn't look much like anything and he had only drawn it from above, not the side too, so he couldn't show the landing gear properly. Billie smiled to herself.

Gribble came round to collect the drawings.

'You didn't even bother?' he said, looking at Stone's blank sheet of paper.

'The kids can have their stupid bit of shelf.'

***

'Can't we share it?' Tommy said two hours later as Billie bent down to put her pencils in her new pigeon hole.

'Sure, but you'll have to put my name on your post. "To Tommy, care of Billie Swift, White Waltham Airfield,"' she gloated.

Tommy didn't look too happy about this. He looked at the typed label on the bottom-most pigeon hole. 'It's not fair, I've worked here the longest.'

'It doesn't matter,' Billie sighed. 'They won't let us keep it for long.'

They both knew who the pigeon hole had belonged to. Prince Suprabhat Chirasakti of Siam who had left White Waltham in the Summer and joined the pool at Kirkbride. He had perished there soon after. Billie had never met him, but had overheard many of the pilots sorrowfully reminiscing about him. He'd got stuck in the Dumfries valley full of cloud and flown his Hurricane into the side of a mountain.

But this tragedy, like all wartime disasters, was only spoken of in a hushed whisper. Nobody cried in public. Not even the American pilots like Nancy, who were mocked for being soppy and sentimental. Very rarely did they openly talk about lost comrades. The only time it had come up was when Billie had overheard Diana in the briefing room complaining that the men were paid more than the women were.

'We are safer than the men. Far fewer deaths and crashes,' she sniffed.

'What about Amy Johnson?' Billie knew her hero had died a couple of years ago. Her obituary was the most exciting one Billie had ever read. She'd done amazing things, even flown solo from London to Australia, but had died in the UK over a year ago, working for the ATA.

'I was out in the same weather that day, but I was lucky,' Jackie said. 'The fog moved in quickly. She must have done what I did and flown above the clouds. She was meant to head for Oxford. I had an easier route, or maybe I was more gung-ho. I flew blind back down through the cloud.'

'You could have hit a hill!' Nancy said in disbelief, 'or a balloon. That was really dangerous.'

'I know, but I was flying in circles looking for a break in the clouds. I didn't have any fuel left. It was scary,' Jackie said. 'What Amy did was far more sensible. She ejected out of her plane, so yes, the plane was lost, but she should have been safe...'

'But she didn't know she was over the Thames estuary,' Diana said, shuddering a little. 'If she had been anywhere else, she would have landed, and made her way back to her ferry pool. Instead, she drowned in the water with the captain of the boat who tried to rescue her. It really is sad.'

Fairweather turned to Jopp and said, 'You'd think that women would be more cautious than us. I always assumed that's why they had a better record than the men.'

'Do they?' Billie asked.

'Apparently so, fewer crashes at any rate.'

'It's because the planes they fly are easier,' Stone said, striding into the room. 'Ops doesn't like to give women difficult planes and they aren't allowed to fly the large bombers like the Lancaster.'

'Yet,' Lettice Curtis said coolly.

'I've thrown three Walruses this month,' Anna said. 'They are awful.'

'You don't have to fly class six either.'

'What are class six?' Billie asked

'Sea planes,' Nancy said. 'And the reason we don't fly them is because none of us want to get stuck in a storm having to share accommodation with a crew of drunken sailors.'

Fairweather leant forward. 'So tell me, why do women make better pilots?'

'Because we are the cream of the crop,' Lettice said. 'Most of us were flying before the war, and racked up hundreds of hours. Most of us are still young.'

'You boys are all old and tattered RAF rejects,' Nancy laughed.

'With missing parts,' said Jopp pointing to his missing arm.

Billie watched Stone's face pinch into a scowl.

CHAPTER TWENTY-TWO

Two days after Billie had won her pigeon hole, she was surprised to see a brown parcel in it.

'To Bill

P28 Air Transport Auxiliary

No.1 Ferry Pool

White Waltham

HANDLE WITH CARE'

It wasn't heavy. Billie gently turned it over in her hands. It felt familiar. She carefully removed the brown paper without tearing it, a habit that she'd copied from her mother. The blank box had another box inside it. Billie immediately recognised the pressed pulp and familiar shape of a half dozen egg carton.

She opened it and inside were six brown eggs. They weren't clean, but that didn't matter.

A note had stuck itself to the inside of the lid. She peeled it off. It was typed.

Be a good egg. Don't tell tales. If you'd like more put the box back in your pigeon hole overnight.

She looked around. Six eggs. She didn't even think about it. She ran straight to Ralph.

He was already by the hen coops.

'Alright trouble?'

'I got the eggs,' she panted. 'Sorry it took so long.'

'Did it work?'

'Yes!' Billie said happily. 'My mother isn't going to murder Susan.'

Ralph, who had no idea who Susan was or why this had anything to do with eggs, nodded and took the eggs.

Billie ran back into the briefing room and placed the box back in her pigeon hole. She couldn't wait to tell Susan that all their problems were over.

Susan, however, wasn't in the mood to chat. For some reason she seemed to disapprove of Billie. Very few eggs had been laid. It was two weeks since the plane crash. Billie didn't understand why Susan hadn't recovered from the shock by now.

It didn't matter anyway. If the mystery egg giver kept their promise and gave Billie another refill, Billie's mother would never know.

Susan eyed her as she opened up the coop to look inside.

'Why aren't you saying hello?' Billie asked. 'Harris is being friendly.'

Susan turned her back.

'Hey, I've saved you from the chop!' Billie said, prodding her.

Susan ignored her.

She shut the coop, annoyed that her good mood had been spoilt by Susan being all judgemental. It didn't occur to Billie that Susan couldn't have known about the mystery egg benefactor. She was a hen. She had no idea that Billie was effectively accepting a bribe. But it was hardly a bribe. All she had to do was not tell tales. That was easy enough, wasn't it?

***

On Wednesday flights were delayed so that the pilots and ground crew could attend the Armistice Day service at the church. Mrs Swift had a shift so wasn't there. Billie had gone to the airfield, and been delighted to find that the egg box was full again. She collected her box of mystery eggs and put them all in her chicken coup before heading to the church. They would be there for her mother to find when she got back in the mid-afternoon.

Her mother might not be in church but the school was. Billie's classmates all lined up. She saw a couple stare and whisper. Mr Hart in particular looked confused as she marched with Tommy to the front with the rest of the ATA. All the pews were taken.

It had been over twenty years since the end of the Great War and that seemed like ancient history. But in the last couple of years, the poppies and prayers felt more real. Especially when Michael was locked up somewhere, only writing every few months.

The whole church sang together:

'Lord of all might, thou God of love
Whose throne is in the heights above.
The wind thou holdest in thy hand,
The lightnings move at thy command
Look down in mercy; hear our prayer
For those in peril in the air.'

Bill's eyes were on Stone, watching him sing next to other RAF officers in full uniform, knowing he was up to something. Spitfires were a symbol of hope and bravery. He'd crashed one, and then set light to it. It felt like sacrilege.

'Their escort be; their guardian strong,
As through the skies they speed along.
Through clouds and storms and
    trackless space
Guide and uphold them with thy grace.
Look down in mercy; hear our prayer
For those in peril in the air.'

He turned and caught her staring at him. His smug expression changed into confusion. A hatred burned through Billie that she couldn't help but whisper:

'Look down in mercy; hear our prayer

But not for him in the air.'

On the way out of church, Mr Hart called Billie over. Her heart sped up as she glanced over at the two police constables who were collecting their bicycles which were resting against the side of the building. Her hatred of Stone was replaced by a sudden realisation that Mr Hart could have her arrested as a truant.

'Why aren't you in school?'

'I am,' Billie said quickly. 'I'm having lessons at the ATA.'

'Flying lessons?'

'And meteorology, mechanical engineering…'

Mr Hart's eyebrows raised. 'Your mother never said you would be…'

'She's busy with the ambulance,' Billie cut him off.

'Everything alright Billie?' said Nancy.

'Yes,' Billie said, happy to stop the interrogation before it started. 'This is my old teacher.'

'Morning,' Mr Hart said touching his hat. 'Billie says she's taking classes at the airfield?'

'That's right, she's a cadet.'

Mr Hart paused. He had a look of confusion on his face.

'Nancy Bamford.' Nancy held out her hand. 'Second Officer, ATA.'

'You're American?'

'Guilty as charged. What's your name?'

Mr Hart was taken aback by her rudeness. 'Hart, Cuthbert Hart. I know. Bit of a mouthful. That's the one advantage of being a woman of course.'

'What is?'

'You can marry a man with a decent last name. I'm stuck with mine.'

'I've heard worse methods of picking a husband,' Nancy mused. 'But you can still change your name, legally I mean.'

'Can you?'

'Oh yes, I knew a man who had to change his name. He thought about it for a while but when the war started, he just had to.'

'What was his name?'

'Adolf Stinkbottom.'

Billie and Mr Hart chuckled.

'What did he change it to?'

'Morgan Stinkbottom.'

Billie and Mr Hart laughed again.

'Good one,' Mr Hart said.

'Nice to meet you Mr Hart.'

'You too Miss Bamford.'

Nancy took Billie by the arm and walked with her out of the church.

'How do you do that?' Billie asked

'Do what?'

'Make friends like that,' Billie said.

'Probably my accent,' Nancy said. 'I shouldn't speak ill of your countrymen but they are as snobby as they come. Back home I wasn't exactly living in the high cotton but I could still rub along with just about anyone. So can most folks. But on this side of the pond it matters how you talk. You can be the most successful man or most beautiful lady to ever walk the earth but when y'all hear a dialect, you get cut off before you can start.'

Billie recalled how the evacuees were forced to repeat themselves by the adults.

'Ber ah do toor pwop-pah,' one had shouted back. He was forced to wash his mouth out with soap and water, a punishment usually only reserved for children who swore.

'But you have an accent,' Billie said.

'Yes. They can't figure out where to put me. Between you and me most of the gals in the ATA are upper class knuckleheads. I love them,' she quickly said. 'But getting on their good side was a chore.'

'You like Diana though,' Billie said.

'Of course,' Nancy grinned. 'But she's half-American.'

'Is she?'

'Yes, and she isn't a snob. It's why I like you, Bill,' Nancy said. 'You're not dazzled by ranks, RAF uniforms or the proper way to do things. You don't even care how you look or come across when you talk. You care about the important stuff.'

Billie thought for a moment. 'Like stalling speeds?'

'Exactly.'

CHAPTER TWENTY-THREE

Billie knew Stone had said on the phone that he would make a 'drop' on Friday the thirteenth. That was today and Billie was determined not to let him out of her sight.

'Good morning,' Chile greeted her.

'Where are the boys?'

'Tommy is late. Stone is in taxi plane.'

Billie frowned. 'But Stone isn't allowed to fly until he completes this course!'

Chile shrugged. 'The war changes rules.'

'Did you see his chit?'

Chile shook her head. 'No.'

'So you don't know if he really has got a plane to deliver?'

'He is in taxi plane, so he has chit.'

'Has it left yet?'

Chile shrugged.

Billie had to see if it was true. She ran out of the classroom and down the long corridor.

She made it out the building and saw the Anson's engines begin to start up. She was too late... she ran to the plane, and, when she got within fifty feet it began to taxi. As it moved past, Lettice, Fairweather, Anna and Jackie all waved at her through the window. Sat at the back, Stone caught her eye and flicked her the V.

The taxi plane was late returning. Billie had finished lunch by the time Nancy came in.

'Stone not with you?' Billie asked.

'No, he should be back here by now. He was only flying a Spit from Abingdon to Witney.'

'I thought he was grounded?' Lettice asked.

'He is for the ATA,' Diana said crisply. 'But not the RAF.'

'He's delivering a Spit for the RAF?'

'It must have some top-secret gear aboard that they don't want us knowing about,' Diana said wisely. 'Cameras and the like I expect. Pilot likely has to be non-civilian.'

Anna tutted. 'So he gets to fly a lovely Spit and I had to ferry a damn Walrus.'

'But he should be back by now?' Billie asked.

'We've probably missed him.'

'His car is still here,' Billie said pointedly. She'd been checking on it during Gribble's afternoon lesson. He must think she had an upset stomach.

'That is a very nice car,' Nancy said dreamily.

'I don't know how he affords to run it,' Diana said. 'My papa only takes the Bentley out once a week to pick up a fish crate full of leftovers from the fishmonger. That one trip guzzles all his petrol ration just to fulfil his chitterling addiction. A sports car like that… Stone must be getting extra coupons from somewhere.'

Billie listened intently. Stone was getting extra petrol rations? How? Maybe being an RAF officer got you extra petrol. Or maybe being a Nazi spy did. The idea that he was being trusted with a top-secret airplane was troubling. What if he gave away its secrets?

'Your dad's a racing car driver, isn't he?' Nancy asked Diana.

'He was. Now he's a wing commander like Cummings. My mother is running a farm. It's jolly impressive,' Diana said.

'My mother is an ambulance driver,' Billie said brightly.

'I never learnt to drive,' Nancy said.

'But you're American!' Diana protested. 'I thought firing a gun and driving a truck was your version of a Bat Mitzvah.'

'I'd been fixin' to. But I've five brothers.'

'That explains why you aren't married,' Pauline Gower said, as she strode into the mess.

'Southern men are born gentlemen, plain spoken, but you can always hitch a lift without trouble,' Nancy said wisely.

'We'll have to give you driving lessons,' Diana said. 'Seems ridiculous that you can fly a Blenheim and be unable to drive a motor car.'

'I should take Stone's roadster for a spin. I'm sure he wouldn't mind,' laughed Nancy.

'If only we could,' said Diana with a hint of jealousy. 'It is such a beautiful car. And the rotter leaves his keys out in the open to tempt us all with.'

Billie looked over to the side table where Diana was pointing. On it was Stone's green scarf, leather driving gloves, cigarette packet, and keys. They glinted.

Billie knew what she was about to do was wrong. It was incredibly naughty. But she was a naughty girl, so it was to be expected.

She slowly made her way towards the keys while the adults continued to chat. It wasn't stealing. She was borrowing the keys. She only wanted to snoop in his car. She wouldn't take anything. Not unless she found a letter addressed to Hitler in Berlin or something.

She faced the group and backed slowly into the corner. She bumped into the side table, and felt around behind her for the metal keys nestled among the leather and wool. She had them. She stayed still for a moment while Diana told another anecdote about doing a barrel roll in a Spitfire and her make-up powder falling up into the fuselage and bursting open. She hadn't been able to reach it and had righted the plane so that the make-up powder had coated her and the cockpit in beige dust.

'Always button up your top pocket,' she said sagely.

Everyone was laughing too hard to notice Billie slip out of the mess.

Because she hadn't wished to draw attention to herself, Billie hadn't taken her coat. The cold air pierced through her cardigan, making her crouch to keep warm. This hid her from view from the offices as she moved quickly behind the row of cars. Her feet barely crunched on the sparse gravel on the drive.

It was obvious which car Stone's was. The red one.

Its leather roof was up. With numb fingers, Billie put the key in the driver's door lock and turned it. She quickly climbed inside and shut the door behind her. She looked out of the windows, triple-checking to see if anyone had followed her.

No one was coming. The car was a mess. The front seat was covered in empty cigarette packets, a bottle of whiskey, a jumper, newspaper, a pocket magazine called Lilliput, a pen, a half-eaten chocolate bar which Billie wanted to take for herself, and one sock with a hole in. No notes, no secret letters. It was strange. Every grown-up that Billie knew had post on them, in their handbag, their briefcase, their car, their kitchen table. Where were the old telegrams and the scribbled-on envelopes? She felt down the crack of the seat and uncovered an old betting slip and a half crown coin. Her mission had come to nothing.

After checking the foot wells, Billie shook out the jumper and flipped through the magazine. Finally. a bit of hope. A note was tucked inside. What was written on it made no sense. It was a list.

At first glance it looked like a list of women's underwear. Billie studied it more closely. Some of the words were spelt incorrectly.

'Slips – 10. R-on,' she muttered to herself, her eyebrows knotted.

The numbers didn't refer to a size. It seemed unlikely that Stone needed twenty brassieres. Next to the word 'girdle' were things that looked very suspicious indeed: 'secret helper', 'French line'. These items must refer to something else.

She thought about how many planes were delivered by the ATA. Were they names of airfields? Could the number refer to a date or grid reference?

Billie took out her pencil and as fast as she could she made an exact copy on a scrap of paper she had in her pocket. She was careful to mark every detail from the bad spelling to the crossed-out words.

She slipped the list back into the magazine and got out of the car.

It was then she noticed the round bump for the spare tyre at the back of the vehicle. It too had a handle and key. Trust Stone to hoard a rationed rubber tyre… unless… she went to open the hatch. It fell open and inside wasn't a spare tyre. At first Billie thought it was bed sheets until she realised. It was a parachute. But if Stone's parachute was here, what was in his parachute bag?

CHAPTER TWENTY-FOUR

When Billie got home, she went straight to the bookcase behind the radio. Billie's father treated his books like they were chickens. They were precious. Perhaps it was because she wasn't allowed to go near them that Billie had been so keen to start her own collection in her bedroom. And why she had gone for books with similar titles to her dad's and not the stupid fairy tales or books about horses her mother kept suggesting she read. Her father was particularly adamant no one go near his encyclopaedias but it wasn't those that Billie wanted. She wanted a small book that had often intrigued her as a small child. It was called *Secret Writing* and promised to teach you how to write and decipher different codes.

While her mother was in the kitchen, Billie gently lifted the book off the shelf. The gap it left toppled the rest of the books on the shelf so they all leant to the right. Billie double-checked to make sure her mum was distracted, went upstairs and grabbed her copy of *Black Beauty* that she had been using as a coaster on her chest of drawers, and swapped the books' dustjackets. She then placed *Black Beauty* onto the shelf. Once everything looked back to normal, she sat on the armchair and read feverishly.

'What are you so absorbed by?' her mother interrupted.

Billie held up the book with the *Black Beauty* dust jacket disguise.

'There you go, I knew you'd like it!' Billie's mother beamed. 'I've got to leave for work now – another night shift. I'll see you tomorrow after school.'

'Uh huh,' Billie said.

'Have some soup. It smells like feet but it tastes good.'

Billie nodded and began on cryptography basics. The Julius Caesar code…

***

Billie woke up in the dark and fell off the sofa. She could hear Susan pecking on the kitchen window. It was pitch black in the house, as the curtains were still up. She was so cold the kitchen tiles didn't bite at her feet like they usually did. She felt around and unbolted the back door. It was only just dawn. Susan ran into the house, flapping up onto the table, looking for crumbs.

She was late at the airfield; it was already eight thirty by the time she left the house with a slice of national loaf between her teeth. She ran, jumping over the pothole puddles.

By the time she had spilled into the building, the hit of warm air caused her to cough. She collapsed against the wall in the briefing room. Evidently the chits were late as every chair was taken with bored pilots waiting to fly.

Nancy waved at her. 'Hey Billie, this will dill your pickle.'

'It will what?' sneered Stone.

'I'm fixin' to take a plane to Burtonwood. Just waiting on the weather. I'd sure welcome company.'

'Wather you than me,' Wamsay warned. 'That Battle gave me no end of pwoblems.'

'Take a hot water bottle or two with you,' advised Lettice. 'I don't know if it's just the glass, but I think they're colder than other planes.'

'What you ladies want is a go in that Lancaster bomber we've got stuffing up the hangar. They have a heater right by the pilot's feet,' said Cummings.

Billie wondered why Cummings was there. Had Stone gotten in trouble again?

'Those are four engines,' Lettice said curtly.

'You'll all be trained up for those in no time. It'll be like the single fighters. Once one of you has proven she can do it, they won't stop the rest of you getting your class fours.'

'And what if I make a mistake and don't pass?' asked Lettice.

'Well.' His moustache twitched. 'Don't.'

'No pressure on me then,' Lettice said sarcastically and continued to read her paper.

CHAPTER TWENTY-FIVE

The Battle that Nancy and Billie were to be flying was in the very worst condition it was possible for a plane to be in. Wamsay had picked it up yesterday from an airfield in Kent. She was supposed to have flown it to be scrapped but the weather had forced her to land at White Waltham. Technically that was supposed to have been its last flight.

Today would be its final flight.

Billie had never seen so many parts marked U/S on the paperwork. Evidently this plane has been through the wars. Quite literally, going by the bullet hole on the rudder.

Billie had the unnerving task of sitting in the rear gunner's seat. Sitting facing the rudder was a bit strange but not as deeply bizarre as taking off backwards.

Nancy powered the Battle's Merlin engine. The glass above Billie rattled. So did the panelling. So did her head. Lettice was right. It was bitterly cold. However, nothing could stop Billie grinning from ear to ear as the engine roared and she was jolted forward. It wasn't as fast a take-off as the Anson because the Battle only had one engine. A rather sickly sounding one. The countryside slid past. Perhaps it was the drone of the engine or the throbbing fuselage or even that she hadn't slept well on the sofa last night, but Billie quickly fell asleep.

She didn't wake up until she heard the engine whine drop sharply. It coughed. Then the engine stopped. There was a brief moment when Billie recalled the sudden silence of the Spitfire falling overhead, before the whole plane tipped up as Nancy directed it straight for the ground.

'Don't pitch a fit!' Nancy's voice said down the speaking tube. 'I've got her.'

Billie knew what Nancy was doing. By diving the plane at the ground, she was maintaining its speed and stopping it from stalling. It was frightening. Billie hoped Nancy was looking around for somewhere safe to do a forced landing: a field or even a nearby airfield. The silence was eerie, only broken by minor turbulence.

All Billie could see was the vast blue above her as the plane continued to dive.

She thought for a moment about the hymn they'd sung in church. She wished that God's hands would reach down to catch them. Just when she expected Nancy to tell her to brace for landing, the engine roared back into life. Billie was comforted by a view of the countryside as they shot up again.

Above the noise of the engine, Billie could hear Nancy laughing.

It wasn't too long before they made a more controlled descent. They joined a circuit and Billie could see other aircraft in the distance, all queuing patiently. As the plane banked, Billie's jaw dropped. It was the largest airfield she'd ever seen. The runways were concrete, almost double the length of the strip at White Waltham and at least triple the width. There were planes everywhere: some in bits, some fighters parked in groups. Hangars cluttered the landscape.

Billie could tell that the Battle was hard to fly. Every now and then the plane would drop and swoop up again. Billie held onto her belt, trying not to think of which bit of fuselage she would smack into if it were to stall entirely. She twisted her head to see that the flaps were all the way up. As they got lower, Billie watched the rudder in front of her move this way and that. The crosswind was obviously strong. The whole plane shuddered as though trying to scramble its occupants.

Landing backwards was bizarre. Billie watched as the runway grew in length in front of her. Surely they would run out of space. To her immense relief, they touched down. The plane was still fighting with Nancy. It wanted to take off again. It reminded Billie of a struggling chicken, itching to be let go. They bumped a few times, the landing gear moaning underneath them.

'Sorry,' Nancy shouted down the speaking tube. 'The dials are catawampus.'

They taxied up to the nearest hangar and Billie watched as another plane landed just moments behind them.

Billie got out of the aircraft. A crowd of American soldiers gathered around Nancy like chickens at a feeder. They were all tall but had baby faces. Some looked the same age as Tommy. Billie had only ever seen this many Americans in the cinema. She half-expected them to start singing and dancing.

'Who is this?' A young man with blond hair waved at Billie as she dropped down onto the wing and rather haphazardly flopped down to the ground.

'I'm Billie,' said Billie to the surrounding boys.

'Hey, she's English!'

'You dolls aren't USAF?'

'We're ATA,' Billie said.

'Ata girls,' they laughed.

'The Air Force won't let us fly with you guys,' Nancy said. 'So me and the girls got on a boat and came here.'

'You didn't marry a Brit did ya?'

'I'm not married.'

'I'm sure we can do something about that!'

They laughed.

'Excuse me gentlemen.' A man in an RAF ground crew uniform approached. The Americans reeled back.

'Can I help you, boy?'

It seemed strange that they called him boy, when he looked a little older than most of them. The man had dark skin and a thick Jamaican accent. 'This one needs taking to the Mary Ann site.'

The soldiers weren't directly rude to the man but it was clear they were put out by his interruption. Nancy also seemed distant with him.

'Do you need the chit? Billie should have it.'

'Where be Billie?' he asked, looking around the group.

'Over here,' Billie waved. She put down her parachute and withdrew the pink chit from her pocket.

'Wah gwan,' the man said. 'Billie is an odd name for a girl.'

'Yes, sir,' she smiled, handing him the chit.

'You're a right raggamuffin,' he said. 'How old be you?'

'That's top secret.'

He laughed.

This proved too much for one of the Americans who snapped, 'You take your own sweet time, won't you boy?'

The man pretended to pay no attention to the American and continued to focus on Billie. 'Can you get me the snag sheet?'

'Here it is,' Nancy said, handing it to him.

'No airspeed indicator. You landed ok?'

Nancy nodded.

'Impressive,' he said.

'Hey.' The American wasn't smiling. 'I said take the plane.'

'I think these gentlemen are right,' the man said. There was something in the way he said 'gentlemen' that made the word sound like 'pig slop'. 'It's about time we get moving.'

He stepped up on the plane wing. 'Nice to meet you, Billie.'

'Nice to meet you too Captain…?'

He laughed, 'Mi a technician. Herbert, Herbert Greaves.'

'This guy is slow as molasses,' one of the Americans said.

Herbert ignored the men. 'Mi see yuh likkle more den, Billie.'

'Can you show us where we can rest up?' asked Nancy to the nearest soldier, who was still eyeing Herbert with suspicion.

'Sure, let me get the car.'

CHAPTER TWENTY-SIX

You'd never start a car up for such a walkable trip in White Waltham, Billie thought to herself as they drove to a hut with a sign that read, 'Spamteria'. The number of planes in the air or engines being tested drowned out the casual conversation as they entered the shabby building. It was the first time Billie had seen a 'Whites Only' sign.

Nancy had selected the most 'corn fed' GI to sit with them. Billie watched them both eat with interest. They held their forks the wrong way up. Randy in particular didn't even bother with a knife and used his fork in the wrong hand to slice up his food as well as shovel. Billie somewhat identified with the knife. They were both sitting there waiting for something useful to do.

While the two Americans exchanged pleasantries, Billie filled her boots with food. She wasn't too keen on the cola but was impressed by the two tinned pork chops, creamed corn, 'biscuits' and peanut butter. She even had a second serving of ice cream with maple syrup.

'Real coffee. It has been *too* long,' Nancy breathed into her mug.

'You can have some nylons if you like,' Randy smiled.

'They give you women's stockings?' Billie asked, thinking it an odd addition to a military ration.

'You should save those for a sweetheart,' Nancy said.

'I don't like English girls,' he said before turning to Billie. 'No offence.'

'None taken,' mumbled Billie as her tongue was stuck to the roof of her mouth with peanut butter. She spotted a troupe of Black men walking outside in uniform. After meeting Herbert, she was confused. 'Are they British? Or American?'

'Yeah, they are GIs.' Randy smiled, tugging on his sleeve. 'Same uniform.'

'Why are they all together?'

'Where we're from, we don't mix races like you do here,' said Nancy.

'The clubs in Warrington are a real mix,' Randy said, scandalously. 'There are local girls here who dance with them. White girls I mean.'

'Pa would be so cross with me if I did that,' Nancy said somewhat sadly.

'Why?' asked Billie.

'It's like putting your underpants on over your britches,' Randy shrugged. 'People would say y'all strange dancing with Black folks. And they'd probably say the same about dancing with white folks.'

'Would they?' asked Billie.

'I dunno, I ain't asked them.'

'What about Herbert?' asked Billie.

'Who?'

'The technician,' Billie said. 'He was Black but he wasn't American. He's Jamaican.'

'I think the rule still applies...' said Nancy somewhat uncertainly. 'If he was in Tennessee, he'd have to use different entrances.'

'That isn't fair,' Billie said flatly. 'I'm not American and I can eat here, but he can't?'

'It's just the way it is,' Randy shrugged. 'This airbase is big. Everyone can make their own friends. Probably more of his kind here than in all of Liverpool.'

'There, you see?' Nancy smiled.

Billie was confused. It wasn't as though British people weren't also rude to Black people but after Nancy's vocal dislike of British snobbery, it surprised Billie that Nancy seemed to accept this particular bias. Billie thought it best to leave the subject alone.

'How come the base is so big?'

'We're making use of the docks, the planes come in bits on boats and we haul 'em here and fit 'em.'

'Why not build them in America and fly them here?'

'Across the Atlantic? They're fighter planes!'

Billie felt stupid. Of course, they couldn't do long distance without refuelling. The longest you could probably fly a Spitfire was to Scotland.

'Why not have the base in Liverpool itself?'

'Too many eggs in one basket?' Randy shrugged. 'Unlikely they'd bomb here and the docks on the same day.'

'Do you get bombed often?'

'We love raids! Shot a Dornier down last week! If brains were leather, the Nazis wouldn't have enough to saddle a junebug,' he laughed. 'We're looking at the sky! They'd do more damage sugaring the fuel or setting fire to a hangar. Place a stick of dynamite in ops we'd be runnin' like a chicken with its head cut off.'

'Don't. Ya'll give me conniptions,' Nancy gasped.

'It won't happen,' he said reassuringly. 'Hitler hasn't got the sense God gave a goose. He'd need someone on the inside and any man who went against the US Air Force would be so dumb he could fall at the ground and miss.'

Falling at the ground and missing... to Billie that sounded like a pilot.

CHAPTER TWENTY-SEVEN

'Are you two gossiping again?' Billie's mother said, bending down under the kitchen table to see Billie, crossed legged on the floor, with Susan puffed up on her lap. 'Careless talk costs lives.'

'What would we know that Hitler would be interested in?' Billie asked.

Susan clucked in agreement.

'Very well, but you'll be late for school if you don't get a wiggle on,' Mrs Swift said. 'String-bean, I know you are fond of the chickens...'

'Not again,' said Billie from under the table. 'You said that if they started laying again you wouldn't touch them.'

'I know I did, but after those two clutches a few weeks ago, the supply isn't exactly forthcoming. We were down to two this morning.'

Billie grimaced. She'd only got three eggs from her mystery benefactor last week. The empty egg box sat hopefully in her pigeon hole but was yet to be refilled.

Billie covered Susan's ears and whispered. 'If you kill a chicken, I refuse to eat any of it. Not a bite.'

'You best hope they start laying again because I'm not eating rabbit on Christmas Day.'

She left for work and Billie had to rush to put Susan back in the run and get changed into her ATA gear. When Billie arrived at the airfield, Nancy and the rest of the pilots had already left in the taxi plane.

Randy's words echoed round her brain. What if Stone wasn't just spying? What if he was going to commit sabotage? After all, better to attack the civilian ATA than the RAF who were armed to the teeth. The ATA was the soft underbelly to Britain's war effort. Attack the ATA and the planes would never get from the factories to the airbases. Without planes Britain's defences would crumble.

If only Billie could work out what exactly Stone was planning. How was she supposed to do that when she had to go to class?

Gribble's mood was like Susan's when she was feeling broody. He was fluffed up and couldn't tolerate anyone too close to him. Billie noticed he was drinking a lot of water. It probably had something to do with a Christmas party that had occurred last night.

He told them to copy out the key of the OS map so they were familiar with the different symbols and lines and could recognise them at a glance.

Billie finished this task quickly and, rather than bother Gribble for something else to do, she opened the back of her exercise book and worked some more on deciphering the code she had found in Stone 's car. She had to be careful; Stone was at the back of the class, also nursing a hangover.

The code was impossible. The words and the numbers made no sense. She'd already tried rearranging the letters and even played around with Playfair ciphers, missing out the most obvious letters. The trouble was, the words she had weren't gibberish and they were followed with a double-digit number. They looked like normal words that made no sense in context. She wasn't sure of the meaning for all of them.

'Sir?' she held up her hand.

Gribble grunted.

'What is a slip?'

She had to be careful. She didn't want to arouse Stone's suspicions. But he was reading a magazine and paying no attention anyway.

'It's a vest, isn't it?' said Tommy.

'Stupid boy,' Gribble snapped. 'It is a flight manoeuvre. When the aircraft slides sideways in the air.'

So what did 'Slips - 10. R-on' mean? Was it the degree that you wanted to slip or the number of times you had to slip? And what did 'R' stand for? Radio on? Why write it down?

Hose - 34. Hose? Like a fireman's hose? Maybe it was Hase. Or Hasc. Stone had such awful handwriting she could have been mistaken when she copied it down.

Girdle - 02.

Billie reached over and plucked Chile's English dictionary from off her desk.

'Girdle: an encircling or ringlike structure.'

None of this made any sense. Unless... perhaps it was rhyming slang?

At lunch, Billie went down to the chicken coops to find Ralph. Sure enough, he was there.

'Do you know any Cockney rhyming slang?' Billie asked him.

'A little I suppose.'

'Any idea what 'slips' means?'

'You sure you don't mean slits? Slits in a dress, mess?'

'No, it is definitely slips.'

'Slippery? That's for drugs, so it better not be that.'

Billie sighed. 'A teddy?'

'Teddington Lock is a sock,' Ralph offered. 'Actually, I reckon I made that up. What do you want to know all this for anyway?'

'It doesn't matter.' Billie sighed and looked at the hens. 'Listen I might need to ask you a favour.'

'More eggs, is it?'

'No,' Billie whispered. 'I might have to give you Susan to look after for a few days. Just over Christmas. Mum is threatening to kill her for dinner.'

Ralph opened his mouth as if suddenly realising something. 'Ooooh, Susan is a chicken. I thought she was your daft sister or something.'

'Could she hide out here?'

'You know what chickens are like, pecking order and that. I'm not responsible what our hens will do to her.'

Billie nodded. She knew that Susan was at the top in her small flock. She could get a nasty injury when introduced to a whole new set of hens. But would she rather be in with a chance in a new run or face certain death for the Christmas table?

'Can I think about it?' Billie asked.

'Give me some warning. I'd need to be here to separate them if it gets too violent.' He scratched his chin. 'Couldn't you ask Tommy to shoot a rabbit for your table instead?'

'Mum says she's sick of rabbit...' Billie sighed again. 'Have you ever heard of eating roast chicken?'

'I've had it a few times,' Ralph said. 'They are a cross between a pheasant and a goose. The French eat chicken I think, but only when they're young. The Scots use 'em for soup. They're a bit stringy for anything else.'

Billie looked as though she were going to cry.

Ralph seemed to realise this. 'I know what will cheer you up. Let's get into the hangars and service that Thunderbolt.'

CHAPTER TWENTY-EIGHT

Two days before Christmas, there was a knock on the door. Billie thought it might be Ralph, here to pick up Susan. But she'd told him to sneak around the back. Mrs Swift answered the door.

'Is Billie in?' said a booming Scottish voice.

'It's a bit early for carol singers,' she said.

Billie ran into the hall and saw at the door were Fairweather, Nancy and Tommy.

'Oh Mum,' Billie stuttered, thinking as fast as she could. 'These are the other volunteers, from the Saturday job.'

'That's right. We know Billie from her Home Front work, raising money for the…' Tommy began quickly running out of steam.

'... the scrap paper collection for…' Nancy continued, also floundering.

'... for ARP wardens'...' Tommy continued.

'... boots,' said Fairweather.

Mrs Swift blinked. 'Do ARP wardens have special boots?'

'Yes,' everyone said together.

'And tonight is special because we are going to be presenting the boots to the ARP wardens for Christmas,' Nancy continued.

'Okay,' Mrs Swift said sceptically.

'And considering Billie's outstanding efforts for the ARP warden scrap paper boot collection,' Fairweather said with authority, 'we thought she'd like to spend the evening, and the night, with the ARP wardens as a reward.'

'Don't you work at the airfield?'

'That's right,' Tommy said, 'and we volunteer to make... paper boots.'

'It is amazing what you can do with paper.' Nancy elbowed Tommy to shut up.

Mrs Swift looked suspicious.

'She'll need to wrap up warm. Maybe take a piece to keep her going?' Fairweather prompted.

At once, Mrs Swift jumped into action. 'It'll have to be fish paste, it's all we have.'

'Thanks, Mum.'

'Do any of you need a sandwich?'

They all declined as they walked into the living room.

'Sorry for tellin' fibs to yer mam,' Fairweather whispered. 'But we want to surprise her.'

Tommy whispered in Billie's ear. 'We got your note about Susan.'

'Did Ralph say if you can take her?' Billie said in a hushed tone to Nancy. 'I'm just so worried my mother is going to kill her.'

'We've got a better plan,' Fairweather said confidently.

'I've got a plausible escape story ready to go,' Billie said, glancing over to the kitchen door to make sure her mother was out of earshot. 'I'll leave a trail of her feathers to a badger hole and I'll tell Mum a fox has got her.'

'Don't foxes kill all the chickens they find?'

'I hadn't thought of that. I'll have to think of something else. Something where I don't have to pluck feathers off Susan. She hates that.'

'What if you give yer Mam a Christmas present that will stop her needin' to kill her?'

'Eggs?'

'Even better! We'll explain on the way. Goodbye Mrs Swift!'

Mrs Swift came trotting back in looking worried. 'Here's your sandwich. Stay safe, won't you? I've got my last shift tonight, so I'll leave the key in the usual spot, alright?'

'I won't go far,' Billie said and followed the others up the road, towards the airfield.

Fairweather wobbled on the fence for some time before he heaved his not unsubstantial frame over and disappeared into the darkness. Nancy, Billie and Tommy followed in silence behind. The rest of the airfield was impossible to make out in the blackout; the only thing they had to go on was the ember of Fairweather's cigarette.

They moved quickly. The Home Guard regularly patrolled the airfield at night, looking out for enemy parachutes or night time saboteurs. There was no sign of anyone.

Billie flinched as a ghostly shape appeared alongside them. It was the Anson.

'You two get in the back,' said Nancy.

'Strap in!'

Billie was aware that Nancy had not done the required flight checks on old Annie. It was also unusual for Fairweather, who outranked her, to be co-pilot and what's more, ground crew.

'I think I know where I am,' Nancy said doubtfully.

'Check your altimeter is set,' Fairweather said. He lit his lighter next to the controls so she could see them. 'I already took away your chocks so once you see the fire, get a wiggle on.'

The fire? Billie looked out the window but saw nothing. It was a dark, cloudy night. There was a slight brightness in the far distance which suggested the moon was behind the clouds, but it might just be her eyes playing tricks on her. The only bright light was the red end of Fairweather's lit cigarette reflected in all the windows. Billie could barely make out Tommy or see her hand.

'There!' The cigarette end pointed at something in the distance. It looked more like a candle than a fire.

Without a moment's hesitation, Nancy started the Anson's propellers. The noise was intense. The Annie's entire body shuddered and wheezed as her engines roared. Without a hesitation she was away, taxiing straight ahead and then turning sharply.

'Take off, quick!' Fairweather said as torches flashed at the plane from the distance. 'Aim for the fire!'

Nancy didn't need telling twice. Both the engines churned into a whining blur and they began hurtling into the dark. The back of the plane lifted. There was the sound of gunfire, but it was too late; Annie Anson's nose rose, she left the ground and they were accelerating upwards at a much steeper angle than Billie was used to.

'That's it!' Fairweather said.

The plane had gone straight into the clouds. The fire that had been the only spot of light in the darkness disappeared.

Nancy continued to accelerate but dropped the nose. They were still climbing, lurching and shuddering through the turbulent cloud. Billie knew that they were flying completely blind.

'Seven thousand feet!' Nancy shouted.

'Keep going, we'll be out of them soon!' yelled Fairweather.

Just as he had commanded, the Anson shot out of the cloud and Billie was dazzled by the light. It was scene fit for a Christmas card. The full moon hung high up above amidst a wash of stars. The clouds were pale blue, purple and white, resembling freshly laid snow spread out like a blanket. The moon was so bright Billie could make out the shadow of the plane on top of the sheet of cloud beneath them. It was breathtaking.

'Everyone alright? No one took a bullet?'

'We're good,' Tommy said with a squeak.

Fairweather said something to Nancy, pointing at the gyro and compass before coming back to talk to Billie and Tommy.

'Where are we going?' Billie demanded. Part of her hoped that somehow, even though she had never spoken of her brother or where he was imprisoned, that Nancy and Fairweather had found out and decided to take her and Tommy to rescue him. That would be the best Christmas present her mother could ever get. Her son with her.

'Ireland,' Fairweather grinned.

'But he's not in Ireland,' she began to say…

'Who isn't?'

'Why are we going to Ireland?' Tommy asked.

'The ATA need a pilot to be delivered for a priority ferry job in the morning... and Bamford volunteered. She and Tommy are going to spend the night at the airbase.'

'What?' Tommy said sounding dismayed.

'Cheer up Tommy,' Nancy shouted, 'we get to ride back in a Mosquito.'

Billie was jealous, Mosquitoes were the fastest of the twin engine bombers. They were also made out of wood, which really made Billie interested.

'Can't I go with Nancy?' Billie asked.

'No. She needs muscle looking after her,' Fairweather said somewhat unconvincingly.

Tommy sat up straighter.

'Also, I don't want to risk the boy's life when it is your chicken we are saving.'

Tommy exchanged a wide-eyed glance with Billie, as if to say 'good luck'.

The flight was as long as it was beautiful. The cloud eventually broke up into smaller puffs of blue. Billie could see water below. It was impossibly black but she could make out the odd ship, or maybe they were rocks, dotted about in the ocean thanks to the shining white moonlight. Billie knew of U-boats torpedoing ships as they crossed the Atlantic. She wondered if there were any in Irish waters...

Soon they were over land. Billie didn't spot the airfield until the last second. Nancy made an expert landing and she and Tommy got out on the runway, as men with torches and guns ran up to them. Instantly a fuel truck got to work, and while Fairweather and Nancy went to sign papers, Billie and Tommy watched shivering as the Anson was fed its dinner. When Fairweather returned Billie waved Tommy goodbye and they were airborne again. This time just Billie and Fairweather flying south over the endless fields.

CHAPTER TWENTY-NINE

The Irish either didn't have a blackout or had a not very good one, Billie thought as the plane passed small villages with bright windows. She was certain she saw a lit lamppost or two as they flew out over the open countryside. Here and there were patches of half-melted snow which helped highlight the houses from the hillsides. The fields here seemed tiny in the moonlight. They reminded her of the ones in Derbyshire she and Nancy regularly flew over on the taxi plane runs. Fairweather was guiding them to their destination as if he had a magic to him.

'What do you know about Ireland?'

'The north of Ireland has a few airbases in it… but it's neutral in the war, isn't it?'

'Exactly. And do you know what that means?'

Billie shook her head.

'You don't need a ration book to buy meat there.' Fairweather grinned. 'We're going to fill this plane up with as many Christmas turkeys as we can stuff into it!'

Just then they hit a bank of clouds. They climbed through them. The rules of the ATA were that you should always be flying during daylight hours, in clear weather or below the clouds so you could see where you were headed. This was the exact opposite of what Fairweather was doing.

'Landing through cloud is all about knowing the height of where you are going to land. That is why you need to make sure the altimeter is correct. Where we're landing is three hundred and thirty feet above sea level so, when we come down, we are going to have a generous safety height that is well above that, or else we might hit a tree or a nearby hill. Clouds can go all the way to the ground and become fog, so don't assume you can always fly beneath them.'

Billie nodded, watching the instruments in front of her.

'If you get stuck in cloud, don't panic. Check your instruments, straighten up, and think. Watch your safety height and use your compass to get back on your original course, then slowly turn round onto your reciprocal. Keep the turn shallow. You don't want to bank too sharply and accidentally stall her or lose your head and get lost by over rotating.'

'I'd want to land.'

'The quickest way to break your neck is on the ground. Just leave your throttle setting where it was when you went in and let down in as shallow a dive as you can. Hopefully you'll see a place to do a forced landing. Whatever happens, if you get to your break-off height, the lowest that you can go without risking hitting the ground, and you're still in cloud, then forget it. Get up high again and bail out.'

'If in doubt, bail out,' Billie muttered.

'Our destination should be…' he said, looking for a gap in the cloud. 'Here!'

The landing was bumpy, but that wasn't Fairweather's fault. It was a short runway consisting of three fields which weren't exactly flat. At the end was a farmhouse. Two trucks were parked outside.

While Fairweather went to greet the farmer, Billie jumped out the back of the Anson. She couldn't believe she was in another country. The grass was sugared with frost and crunched under her feet. Without thinking she picked up a small pebble from the path and placed it in her pocket.

She was approached by a woman with a distinct limp. 'Dia dhiut!'

'Thank you,' said Billie after getting kissed on the cheek. She was dragged into the warm farmhouse and given a hot whiskey. It was flavoured with clove and was very sweet. A big improvement on a cup of tea.

Billie wondered what rationing was like in Ireland, that they had meat and spirits to spare, but didn't ask for more when she'd finished her cup. The couple they were meeting seemed young. The woman had twisted her ankle, hence the limp, and the farmer seemed eager for them to depart as fast as possible.

'You paying in punts too?' he said.

'Most of it's dollars,' Fairweather said, handing several rolls of notes over.

The farmer sucked his teeth. 'We agreed dollars. The punt isn't as valuable. I'm trading a lot with the Americans.'

'Ah,' Fairweather said, looking dejected. 'How's about this?'

He held up his watch. 'It's a fine piece. Swiss made.'

'If you're sure?' The farmer frowned. 'I should give you some dollars back. The watch is worth more.'

'Call it a Christmas gift. But we mustn't dawdle any longer.'

The loading of the plane took over an hour. There were so many turkeys to fit into every part of it. The crates were jammed under and perched on top of the seats. Billie squeezed between them and stuffed loose birds in the gaps. They were all wrapped in newspapers that were slightly bloodstained. It smelt like the butcher's shop. There were a few feathers floating about, too.

It was mildly creepy. Billie couldn't help thinking of Susan as she absentmindedly stroked the un-plucked turkey on her lap. Its head was covered in white wax, which added to its ghostly appearance.

'Short runaway. Heavy cargo. This should be fun.'

Fortunately, the wind had picked up so the plane managed to bump over the fields and take off without much difficulty. Although sleepy, Billie stayed awake watching closely as Fairweather chain-smoked. After he finished every cigarette, he put the stub carefully back in his gold cigarette case. It was dark, and he didn't switch on the cabin light to check the instruments. Occasionally he would open his case and count the cigarette stubs. Billie wondered how Fairweather knew where they were going. The endless stretch of grey cloud offered no clue as to what Billie hoped was England beneath it. Gradually the stars disappeared and the sky began to lighten in front of them. The sun was nearly up.

Fairweather removed the latest stub from his mouth and he placed it along with the others in his case. Billie felt the plane start to descend. He let go of the stick, brushed the ash off his coat with both hands, clasped onto the stick again and announced, 'White Waltham!'

Billie couldn't believe it. They were nowhere and then, just like that, he'd found home.

It was a smooth landing in the daybreak of a drab-looking morning. The airfield was completely empty, aside from the rabbits who hopped out of the way of the taxiing Anson.

'How did you do that?' Billie asked. 'You don't have a wristwatch. How did you know we were here when you couldn't see?'

'It takes seven minutes to smoke each cigarette. I smoked twenty-three so I ken how long we'd been flying. Kept us on course, nothing doing. Just don't tell them I've been smoking.'

'Look, there's Ralph!'

Billie was horrified to see that Ralph was with Stone, standing beside a small van.

Ralph busied himself with refuelling Annie Anson while Fairweather went over to the main building.

Stone and Billie unloaded the turkeys and put them in the van.

'These stink to high heaven,' Stone grumbled.

'They're fresh,' Billie assured him.

'Remind me never to go back to a turkey's digs for a drink. Woof!'

'We can't get more in,' Billie called to Ralph who was up on the Anson's wing with the petrol hose. He gave the thumbs up and waved over to Fairweather who was moving back.

'The met report isn't in yet, but according to last night's charts the cloud is here to stay. You'll be fine, just stick to the rules, yeah? I'm not sure about the balloons either so give the towns a wide berth.' Fairweather said to Stone.

'Up to Crosford?'

'Yup, they'll take them from there to the ferry pools. And don't you go keeping one! Yours is marked, it's in the van with mine and Ralph's.'

'As if I'd ever steal!' Stone smiled.

Billie wanted to say she didn't trust him at all. But she watched quietly as he jumped in the Anson and started the engines.

'Here,' said Fairweather, handing Billie a large turkey.

'Thank you!' Billie said.

'If you want to do some good, invite Nancy for Christmas and she'll help you pluck it.'

CHAPTER THIRTY

'I hear you are the one we have to thank for the bird,' Billie's mother said. 'It's huge! I could barely get it in the oven.'

'Oh,' Nancy said, 'It was a joint effort and only slightly naughty of us.'

'Billie didn't say how you came across it.'

'We bought it in Ireland, so no rations required.'

'An Irish turkey and an American house guest! Jolly exciting.' Mrs Swift pushed Nancy inside the already stuffed house.

'Can I do anything to help?'

'Don't you dare!'

Nancy squeezed in past the children in the hall, who followed Nancy and Mrs Swift into the small sitting room. The Christmas tree was only waist high, but paper chains and fresh holly hung from every available beam.

'Sit there and have some port. That's my sister, Silvia, Joan, then there's Dennis her husband, Rosemary who's eight, Daniel just one of the terrible twins! It's a shame Charlie and Michael can't be here...' Mrs Swift caught herself.

'I love the decorations!' Nancy said. 'Newspaper chains.'

'Billie did those, she's a bit of a machine when you give her a task.'

'Where is she?' asked Nancy.

'I'm here,' said Billie coming out from behind the coats and immediately getting pounced on by Rosie.

'I was keeping the port for after the war, but I can't be bothered to wait that long. It's Christmas after all!'

'Only a small one for me,' Nancy said politely.

'Where in America are you from?'

'Tennessee,' Nancy said. 'I lived a while in Alabama. Bam Bam Bamford, is what they called me in high school.'

'I liked school. Billie doesn't of course,' Mrs Swift sighed.

Nancy glanced at Billie in confusion. 'You didn't like school?'

'Only a year and a half left, then we need to decide what she should do,' Billie's mother said.

Billie eyed Nancy's face, which was slowly processing what Mrs Swift was saying.

'Do you want to meet the chickens?' Billie said quickly.

They went outside and Billie pointed out Harris and Susan, picking at a patch of grass by the wall. Nancy paid no attention.

'You're still in school?'

'Not really,' Billie lied.

'How old are you? Really?' Nancy whispered.

'Nearly thirteen,' Billie mumbled.

'You're twelve?!' Nancy paced on the frosty grass. 'At twelve I wasn't even allowed in an airfield, let alone flying planes!'

'I haven't flown plane,' Billie said.

'I've let you control the Anson often enough.' Nancy looked at Billie again. 'I thought you were young for your age.'

Billie shrugged.

'Do your parents know what you're doing?'

Her eyes widened. 'You can't tell them. My brother is a POW and Mum's paranoid about safety.'

'It's the first commandment. Honour thy father and thy mother.'

'Honouring doesn't mean telling them everything.'

'It means not lying!'

Susan clucked her agreement.

'But you lied to them!' Billie said. 'You told them we were raising money for ARP wardens.'

'That's different, I thought we wanted to surprise them. I didn't know that while we are flying every day, they think you're in school!'

'It's Christmas,' Billie pleaded. 'Don't ruin the day for them. Not in front of the family!'

'I'm not going to tell them but I really think you should.'

Billie's Uncle Dennis came out into the garden.

'Why are you two freezing your knickers off out here? Get in, we're playing blind man's buff and I'm out to break some heirlooms.'

Christmas was definitely not worth saving a month's sugar ration for, Billie thought rather meanly. The turkey was good, and everyone was impressed with the spam stuffing. The grown-ups had all dived on the home-made wine which, by their expressions, tasted terrible but soon had them giggling. Nancy proceeded to have a great time whilst ignoring Billie entirely. The children played noisily. They'd got a skipping rope, deck of cards, some hand-me-down tin soldiers and a home-made doll with a two-tone face because whoever had hand-knitted it had run out of wool. Plus socks, mittens, scarfs, handkerchiefs. Most reworked out of bits of old fabric.

Even Nancy got given a headscarf as a thank you for the turkey. She'd worn it out the door as she left. She'd kept her word and not mentioned anything to Billie's family about her skipping school to work for the ATA. But she also hadn't spoken a single word to Billie. Not even goodbye or Merry Christmas.

This put a downer on Billie's own Christmas presents. She'd got a pocket knife, similar to the one her brother had. There were three blades, a nail file, a can opener and a spike for picking stones out of horses' hooves. She hadn't avoided the knitting and was now the owner of a bright red woolly hat with ear flaps, a bit like a deerstalker.

Her most prized possession that Christmas wasn't a gift. She'd placed it next to Susan's old wing feather on her dresser.

It was a real Irish pebble.

CHAPTER THIRTY-ONE

Billie wasn't sure if Nancy was cold-shouldering her by requesting a transfer or if it was just coincidence. She heard about Nancy going to the all-women's ferry pool in Hamble first thing on Monday morning. It seemed so sudden.

The words of Eleanor Roosevelt kept going through Billie's head. It was her birthday in fifteen days. If she was cleared to do a solo flight before then, and was marked competent, she could write to the First Lady and tell her she had met her challenge. But it was looking unlikely.

Only high priority deliveries were being made due to the terrible weather. This also meant the class's first test flights were on hold until it cleared up. Billie spent her time revising air speeds or joining Tommy, Chile and Stone working with Ralph in the hangars.

On Wednesday morning Billie pinned back the blackout curtains to reveal long shadows cast by the cold winter sun. Her heart raced as she gazed up at the clear blue sky. It would be today.

Just an hour later she was waiting nervously by the row of Tiger Moth biplanes at the side of the hangar.

While Stone took a test flight with Gribble, Billie and Tommy took turns in one of the aircraft, swapping who was up front and who sat behind. The cockpits in both seats were identical, allowing both teacher and pupil to see the controls and for the experienced pilot to take over if anything were to go wrong.

The Tiger Moth was a no fuss plane. The wings were covered in stretched fabric. You had to be careful where to place your feet when you got in, as it was perfectly possible to rip the linen with a misplaced boot. The fuel tank was overhead and the fuel line (a rubber hose) slunk down to the left-hand side of the first cockpit, like a python hanging from a tree. The wing above and the wing below were held together with wire and a flimsy wooden frame.

Stone made another bumpy landing. It was Chile's turn to do a circuit around the airfield.

'You think you two can handle this?' Stone asked.

'Why not?' Tommy said.

'Going up for the first time with old Grumble behind you?' Stone said. 'I don't know if I could have a pilot like that behind me. Not on my first go. He judges your every move. One mistake and you could be banned from flying forever.'

'That's not true,' said Tommy. He sounded worried.

'Not officially. If it were up to Gribble, I wouldn't have a place at the ATA.' He coughed, 'But I'm a war hero. You two are wet behind the ears. If he doesn't see potential in you, you're out. If you're nervous, he'll pick up on that.'

Billie watched as Chile's plane circled perfectly above them.

'Imagine if something went wrong,' Stone said. 'And you froze and he had to take control of the aircraft from the seat behind you. It would be awful.'

At that Tommy shut up and looked nervously at his hands.

'It won't go wrong,' Billie said.

'Loads can go wrong,' Stone smiled.

Tommy didn't say anything. As if to make him more nervous Chile make the smoothest landing Billie had ever seen. Stone pretended not to notice.

It was Tommy's turn. He went around checking the plane with Gribble. Even though it had only just been flown it was important to make all the checks again. He forgot to check the rudder, and Gribble had to remind him.

'He looks nervous,' Chile whispered.

'I thought your landing was brilliant,' Billie said.

'I did all my learning in planes like this in Santiago.'

'Where is Santiago?'

'In Chile,' said Chile.

'Oh!' exclaimed Billie, 'So, you're not called Chile?'

'No, I'm Margot. But there is already a Margot down in Hamble, so I am Chile,' said Chile.

'Why don't they call you Santiago Margot?'

Chile shrugged. 'English people are not creative.'

Billie was so used to being surrounded by foreign voices in the ATA, she had never questioned why they were here and not fighting in their own countries. 'Why are you in England?'

'To fight in the war. At first, they thought I was a spy so I was in jail. Then, after five days, they let me go. I want to fly with the French but they not use women. So the British had me cooking and cleaning but then I hear about ATA. They only let me fly once my English is OK.'

'I think your English is fantastic,' Billie said.

Margot broke into a smile. 'You are kind.'

'I can't speak any Chilean,' Billie said

Margot laughed. 'Nosotras hablamos español en Chile.'

'Nos attras spaniels inch illy?'

'Not bad,' she laughed. There was a loud roar as Tommy prepared to take off.

Both Margot and Billie winced. The Tiger Moth wasn't going fast enough and took a long time to get off the ground. It was so low Billie thought it would run out of space and hit the tree.

'What do the Yanks say? He lacks guts,' Stone laughed.

The plane was listing to the right. The pilots on the ground tilted their heads in sympathy. The plane wobbled a bit, went off course and eventually circled back to re-join the circuit. His landing wasn't great either, the plane wobbled violently from side to side, Billie worried for a moment he'd contact the wings on the ground.

'You're next, Dumbo,' Stone said with a sneer.

Gribble approached with a pale but decidedly relieved Tommy.

'Bit ropey,' he smiled. 'But I did it. You get blown about a bit more than I thought. I was jerking the stick around. It went better when I just used my finger and thumb to hold it, not my whole hand.'

'You did well,' Chile said, patting him on the back.

Tommy handed Billie the leather flying cap. 'He yells at you through this tube. He swears too, so be careful.'

The cap was big, but not ridiculously so. She also put on Tommy's gloves, which were too large, before going with Gribble to walk round the plane.

'Do you want me to test the fuel?' Billie asked.

'I say let us risk it this once.' Gribble smiled. 'You can blame me as your flight instructor.'

After finishing her checks, she hoisted herself into the front seat, pinned the straps together and gave the harness a tug. It seemed safe enough. She attached the speaking tube to the dangling tubes off the side of her helmet.

'Hold back the stick while I start up the engine,' said Gribble. 'Otherwise, the nose will tip forward.'

Billie clenched the stick and flipped the magneto switches up at his signal. The Tiger Moth's engine bubbled into life. Gribble climbed in behind her. Chile pulled the chocks away and they were moving.

'What's with the exaggerated wiggling?' came a voice through the speaking tube behind her.

'Trying to see past her nose,' Billie shouted back. 'I can only just reach the rudder pedals, so I'm lower down than I want to be.'

'We should get you some high heels,' the voice down the tube chuckled. 'Careful now, you're picking up speed and we've got no brakes.'

Billie eased the throttle with her left hand, and made it to the runway.

'H, T, T, M, P, P, F, G, F, U, S,' Billie muttered. It seemed like overkill, as the Tiger Moth was the least complicated plane there was. It was more like a kite with a propeller. It didn't have brakes, flaps, roof, or starter. Instead of the steering wheel yoke of the Anson, it had a stick which controlled the ailerons and the elevators on the tail. It didn't take long for Billie to finish her checks.

'Remember, once we're airborne I can't hear you,' Gribble's voice said down the tube. 'If you need me to take control, I want you to raise your right arm and make a fist and I'll take over. Otherwise, obey my instructions. Off you go.'

With her left hand, Billie opened up the throttle. She had set the trim with the rudder hard to the right to counter the propeller. The engine hummed. She kept a firm eye on the airspeed. Once it reached 40mph, which took no time at all, she pulled the joystick gently towards her, gradually increasing the angle as the ground slipped away.

Billie grinned. The take-off had been nearly as good as Chile's. The moment Billie tried to take in the view, the aircraft tilted and swayed again. It seemed like the slightest breath of wind would set her off. Billie began to understand why the Tiger Moth had a reputation of being able to separate the good pilots from the great ones. It might not be difficult to fly but even the smallest deviations were immediately noticeable.

She levelled out and set the trim. She knew not to get obsessed with the instruments. Getting the trim 'right enough' on a windy day, was probably better than getting it perfect. She banked as they turned in the circuit.

'Good,' Gribble's voice was a sudden reminder she was not alone. 'I want you to do another round and then land.'

Just then Billie noticed a shining dot in the distance. It glistened for a moment in the winter sunshine. She banked again, and the dot became invisible to her. She knew it was another plane, wanting to join the circuit. Unless it was the Luftwaffe about to take pot shots at a little Tiger Moth... She banked again. Her plane was responding beautifully, and she adjusted the rudder to cope with the crosswind while looking out for the other plane. She spotted it again. It couldn't be German; it was huge, like a Lancaster. But it wasn't a British plane. It was American. A Liberator? It was closer...

and low. As though making a landing. Normally aircraft would join the circuit, the imagined racing track above every airfield, before attempting a landing. That way there was a queue so aircraft could take off and land without bumping into each other. This plane was about to queue barge.

'Ok, I want you to make your landing,' came the voice down the tube.

Had Gribble not seen the massive four-engined bomber? Was this part of the test? Billie wanted to point it out to him but didn't, lest he misunderstood her pointing for the signal for him to take over flying. If he hadn't spotted it, they would crash into it.

The Liberator was getting closer; its landing gear was down. She decided to get out of its way, opened up the throttle and took the Tiger Moth into a steep climb.

'What the...' Gribble swore, '... do you think you're playing at?!'

Billie watched the altimeter rise to two thousand feet and levelled off. The enormous plane roared underneath them.

'Crikey,' Gribble's voice was shaky behind her. 'Good call, Swift. Nicely done. Bring her down and level off at seven hundred. Let's go round again.'

Billie did another circuit, watching as the fire crew approached the landed Liberator.

'They've cleared runway. One more circuit to be on the safe side. Then we'll land.'

Billie wasn't even focused on the controls anymore; she was banking harder so she could see the Liberator with the star on its side, taxiing towards the hangars. Gribble wasn't complaining either. Billie played with the throttle, closing it as they made their final turn towards the runway.

The wind had picked up so much, the landing itself was incredibly short. At one point Billie thought they would be blown backwards. It wasn't a perfect landing but it felt pretty smooth. She wasn't really focused on it, her mind wanting to know why the Liberator had been so rude.

'Very nice,' said the voice through the tube. 'Take her back to the others.'

'That was a narrow escape! We thought you hadn't seen it!' Tommy squeaked.

'What was wrong with their plane?' Billie asked.

'One of her engines was feathered.' Chile shrugged. 'Lucky it found somewhere to land I suppose.'

'Nice flying, Gribble,' Stone said. 'That quick climb was smart thinking.'

'Swift flew that one. I was the idiot telling her to fly into the path of the Americans.'

Stone made a noise somewhere between a cough and a grunt.

CHAPTER THIRTY-TWO

On the ground the next morning, Billie spotted Stone hanging around the hangar.

'Hello, Dumbo,' he said, staring up at the enormous Liberator.

'Are you not coming to class?'

'Gribble wants you lot to help me fix her up,' Ralph called, waving from on top of the wing. It was too high for him to jump down from. He made his way to them from a hatch at the top.

'The crew left last night,' he said as he came out of the bomb door at the side, with Tommy in tow. 'She's in a state. Plus, half her paperwork is missing. I'm not familiar with her innards but we can have a tinker this morning.'

'Can't the Americans send round some mechanics to help with her?' asked Bill

'Not on New Year's Eve, no. She's just one ship and they are building hundreds.' Ralph sucked air through his teeth. 'Job one is trying to work out why one of her engines failed. My money is on her auxiliary fuel cell. Now, it's either the transfer unit that is misbehaving or it's a jumpy shut off valve.'

Both Tommy and Billie nodded knowingly, although they had no idea.

'We'll give the engines a basic service. Check for any obvious dents, unusual wear and tear, clean her insides and grease the gizmos. That will let us rule out a few things. Hopefully we'll find the problem then we can all go and celebrate the end of 1942!'

Billie and Tommy spent the morning being handed bits of metal to clean. They took care to wash the filter screens from the inside, checked the oil with their fingers for lumps of metal, put pipe cleaners up the fuel pipes and lightly greased mechanisms (not too much, or it would collect dust).

Billie enjoyed crawling through the Liberator. It had been converted for mail delivery so that the bombardier's gun in the nose was sealed off from the rest of the ship and only accessible through the hatch at the front of the nose. Billie found that while Ralph and Tommy were busy in the bomb bay the fastest way

225

into the plane and the cockpit was to go up through the nose wheel opening. The Liberator was only two and a half feet off the ground and her thin frame easily fitted through the gap. That was how she managed to get everyone their tea, climbing in and out with one cup at a time and crawling along to the bomb bay, or round then up into the cockpit.

Stone spent most of his time in the cockpit, reading the pilots' notes. After lunch he kept going outside to check the sky, as though he was expecting something. This meant it was up to Tommy and Billie to follow Ralph's orders alone as the other fitters and ground crew did routine maintenance on the other planes.

There were a few things wrong with the Liberator. Traces of blue suggested small leaks. One filter was particularly dirty. But nothing that made Ralph shout eureka. This put him in a decidedly bad mood. Tommy got the brunt of it but soon Ralph snapped at Billie.

'Hurry up!'

'I can't unscrew the end of this…'

He snatched it off her. 'This is why this is a man's job and not for someone with twig wrists. You're in the way!'

All this proved too much for Billie. Rage bubbled through her.

'Fine!'

She stomped away.

The briefing room seemed like the obvious option. When she got there the only other person in the room was Jopp.

'Hello,' she said

He looked up over his newspaper. 'Afternoon.'

Billie knew by the tone of his voice and the way he managed to slide lower in his seat that he wasn't looking for a conversation but she started one anyway.

'Why aren't women strong like men?'

He shuffled his paper. 'Unless the woman in question has a propeller, I can't claim any expertise.'

'When you lost your eye and your arm...'

'Yes?'

'Did it hurt?'

He smiled. 'Oh yes. But what really hurt was I wasn't allowed in the air force anymore.'

'Is that why you're in the ATA?'

'Ancient and Tattered Airmen... and women of course,' he tailed off and looked at Billie sharply through his good eye. 'You however are barely a woman. I knew kids like you in the Great War. They fibbed about their age. It didn't end well for them.'

Billie pretended not to hear him.

'Where is everyone?'

'The taxi plane will be back any minute. They all were clucking about seeing in the New Year in London.' He went back to reading his paper. 'Guaranteed fast delivery if there is a party to get to.'

As if his words had summoned them, Billie heard the faint hum of an Anson joining the circuit. If there was a party in London it was guaranteed to be full of excited young pilots, even ones from different ferry pools. Maybe Nancy would be with them.

She left to watch the Anson make its landing. She saw from the shadows in its windows that it was indeed full of pilots. The moment the engines turned off she ran up to meet them.

'G'day Billie!' Wamsay said. 'You going to be naughty tonight?'

'Yeah, come out with us!' Diana said. 'You'll love London. There's hardly any bombs; the locals don't flinch. You can still catch a cab when they're dropping.'

Billie smiled shyly and searched for Nancy. But she wasn't on the plane. Something else was however. 'Isn't that Nancy's overnight bag?'

'Bam Bam?' Diana said, looking over.

'We waved her off from Hamble, didn't we?' Jackie asked.

'She helped me load the post this morning,' Diana said reaching for it. 'She didn't have her overnight with her…'

'Careful Barnato!'

Diana's hand hesitated as it moved towards the bag.

'Whose bag is it?' Fairweather barked. 'No one recognise it?'

There were murmurings of denial.

'Don't touch it.' His voice failed to hide a nervousness that worried Billie.

'Everyone get out. Carefully.'

All the pilots left the plane in confusion.

'What's the hold-up chief?' said one of the ground crew, trotting up to the aircraft.

'There's a mystery bag on board. Can you get the ARP wardens here? And the fire truck out?'

'Rightio.'

'It's probably nothing,' said Fairweather. Though his face looked serious.

As the fire truck came close, Fairweather approached the Anson again and went inside.

He left the aircraft with the bag at double speed. He marched about thirty feet from the plane and gingerly placed the mystery bag in the middle of the grass. He then scampered away from it like a rabbit fleeing Tommy's shotgun.

'The damn thing is ticking!' he said, panting. 'Get back! All of you.'

'Ticking?'

'Faintly but yes.' Fairweather waved at the truck. 'They'll do a controlled explosion.'

'You think it's a bomb?' scoffed Lettice. 'Nancy has gone and packed her bag with explosives and left it in the taxi?'

'Who would want to bomb a plane of pilots?'

Billie remembered what Randy had said in the Spamteria. Sabotage.

'Do we need to take cover?'

They all paced slowly backwards watching as two of the ground crew, this time with their fire attendance jackets on, sent an ARP warden to the bag.

'Let's get back behind this wall,' Jackie said.

'It's only knee high.'

'Everyone lie down. Jackie, Lettice, get everyone indoors to open all the windows, let the blast come through them.' Fairweather ordered.

'What's going on?' It was Stone. 'What are you all doing crawling around on the floor?'

'Will it be that big an explosion?' Jackie asked. 'Shouldn't we get in the shelter?'

'Probably,' Diana said, 'but then we'd miss the fireworks.'

'Explosion?' Stone looked into the distance. 'What the hell are you on about?'

'If it isn't a bomb, then it won't be a big explosion,' Fairweather explained. 'But if it *is* a bomb, it could take our heads off.'

'Lovely.'

'What are you talking about? What is a bomb?'

'They found a bag on the plane. Looks like Nancy's. It's ticking. Stowed where we usually put our parachutes.'

'No!' Stone shouted. He began running towards the bag, as fast as he could. But it was too late.

There was an enormous boom. Stone was knocked off his feet and fell backwards. The bag and its contents had disappeared. It was a few seconds later when the first of the knickers fell to the grass. Smouldering undergarments rained down. Burnt stockings, garters, slips and brassieres fell down from the sky.

Stone stood up, a jumble of pants cascading off him. He had a particularly large bra on his head, falling over his eyes like pilot's goggles. When it finally fell off, he was livid.

CHAPTER THIRTY-THREE

The aftermath of the 'pants bomb' caused what Billie's mother called a 'to do'. All the pilots including Tommy and Billie were marched into the briefing room while the remains of the bag were investigated. Stone looked white as a sheet. Billie knew he had to be behind it. He'd tried to stop them from doing the controlled explosion. The contents of the bag must have cost a fortune. It must've been multiple years' worth of rations. The ticking, it was rumoured, had come from three men's wristwatches, now all broken.

One after the other Pauline Gower and Commander Wills called each pilot in for questioning. Once each pilot came back, they told who was next to go to one of the rooms.

Stone had gone before Billie. In fact, he had been the second to be questioned. It was about thirty minutes before Billie was called to see Pauline Gower, who had taken a table in the canteen.

'Take a seat.' Pauline said

Billie proceeded to tell her side of the story, that she had been helping mend the Liberator but had taken a break to go to the bathroom (she didn't want to admit the truth, that she had run away because Ralph had snapped at her). She had spoken to Jopp, gone out to greet the Anson and spotted the bag.

'I think it was for Stone,' she said quickly.

Pauline raised her eyebrows. 'It was Nancy Bamford's bag.'

'He spent all afternoon looking for the Anson, ask Ralph. He abandoned his post.'

'So did you. And you and Nancy are close.'

'No, it was Stone who…'

'Stone said he caught you stealing eggs.'

Billie at this point felt the house of cards she had built begin to wobble.

'He's lying,' she said.

Pauline's lips tightened.

'He is!' Billie said. 'He was the one stealing the eggs and giving them to me.'

Pauline Gower's mouth hung open. 'What are you talking about?'

'When I got my pigeon hole, which he definitely let me win, by the way, because Chile isn't good at English spelling.' Billie's voice accelerated. She wanted to get the words out of her mouth before reason could stop her. She needed to save Nancy and in order to do that, she had to confess. 'The next day, there was a box of eggs in it, which weren't addressed to me but they had a note in there telling me to keep quiet and if I did, I'd get some more eggs. And I needed the eggs to pay Ralph back because he let me borrow some and then my dad ate them all and Susan still won't lay any.'

Pauline frowned. 'So you don't know who was leaving eggs in your pigeon hole?'

'It has to be Stone,' Billie said firmly. 'I got the eggs the day after I told him I…'

Bill's eyes widened. She shut her mouth quickly and her face flushed.

'Told him what?' Pauline cocked her head. 'This is important. One of our pilots is in serious trouble and if you can help her, you must tell the truth.'

'I saw Stone's accident. I was by the church when he crashed his Spitfire in October. And it wasn't on fire, the engine was off. His forced landing wasn't like anything he told Gribble. I think he set fire to it after it crashed.'

Pauline didn't say anything at first, she sighed. 'I was also young once; I know you think that you're helping Nancy somehow, but you're lying to me.'

'I'm not!'

'You couldn't have seen it crash from where you describe. A farmer witnessed how its engine was on fire and the whole thing was burnt. Stone was lucky to escape with his life.'

'The farmer is lying, they must have moved it and burnt it!'

'Why?' Pauline said. 'Why would multiple people lie about such a thing?'

Billie didn't know.

'I know why you'd lie,' Pauline said. 'You think you can save the career of a friend by casting shadow on someone you have never liked.'

'He's a spy,' Billie said.

Pauline looked like she was going to laugh. 'You think Stone is a Nazi? Have you any evidence?'

'I've seen him listening at doors, I've heard him on the phone talking about dropping packages. He is keeping something strange in his parachute bag...'

If Pauline was interested in Billie's story, she didn't show it. 'Have you thought that maybe his wing commander, I think you've met Cummings, might have noticed if one of his ace pilots was a Nazi? Do you suppose the Nazis themselves might have told him not to shoot down so many of their aircraft?'

Billie jumped up. 'Oh!'

Pauline's eyebrows raised. 'What now?'

'He made this list. It looked like a code... I've been trying to decipher it.' Billie blurted. 'Slips... Teddy... Watch... he hadn't finished making it! It wasn't a code. It was underwear! It was the contents of that bag!'"

Pauline looked confused. 'Do you have this list?'

Billie shook her head. 'I know where it is though. You need to search his car.'

Pauline looked appalled. 'I can't search vehicles because you just remembered you thought you might have seen something. This sounds like fantasy. You've made it quite clear that you and Stone aren't the best of chums. All I need to know is, do you know who put the bag on the Anson?'

'No,' Billie said reluctantly. 'But I bet whoever did was sending it to Stone.'

'Enough,' Pauline snapped. She was getting angry. 'I think you, Gribble and I need to have a sit down together and decide if you really ought to be part of the ATA.'

'What?' Billie's voice was weak.

'If there is any truth to you witnessing an aircraft in distress, crashing, not calling the authorities – and I know you didn't because the first call was from that farmer – then we should really question your competence. You sat in that classroom, you learnt all about how important accident investigation is, that people's lives could be saved – your friends' lives – and you kept quiet and failed to report an accident you witnessed? For a bribe of chicken eggs! What do you think that says about your moral character?'

Billie didn't burst into tears but it was a close-run thing. 'There,' the voice in her head seemed to say. 'Everyone knows you're a bad person. No one believes you. You shouldn't listen to people like Nancy. Lying *is* the only way people will ever like you.'

What was worse than the voice in her head was Pauline's next sentence, 'I think, after today, we can no longer have you working for the ATA. I commend your spirit, and your ability, I really do. But war is not a game. If we can't trust you to tell the truth, how can we trust you with our planes and the lives of our pilots?'

Billie didn't say anything. She nodded. She felt all the hope leave her body. Even if she proved she was telling the truth about it being Stone's bag, Pauline Gower still wouldn't trust her.

Billie, at that moment, knew that she would never be a pilot. But in the cold misery of her heart, a small flicker of purpose remained. She might never be a pilot but she could still clear Nancy's name.

CHAPTER THIRTY-FOUR

Bill's mind was racing. Instead of going straight back to the mess, she went to see if Stone's car was parked at the front of the building. Sure enough, the sports car shone red on the muddy drive. She wondered if the magazine with the list inside was still there.

She bit her lip and pondered getting the car keys from Stone. Was it worth smashing the car window so she could search it again? When she went out to the car, her heart leapt. There, among the rubbish on the front seat: the same old magazine. She hoped the code was still safely tucked inside. She looked around for a rock... but then remembered her Christmas pocket knife and dug for it in her pocket. She tucked her fingernail under the notch at the top of the blade and pulled. It was stiff but, gradually, opened like a book. Just when she thought it was fully unfurled, her fingernail slipped and the blade snapped back like a crocodile. More carefully this time, her hands shaking from cold and excitement, she opened it again.

She had watched Ralph and the ground crew inflate truck and aircraft tyres. They did it to a precise pressure per square inch and would watch the gauge on the pump intensely. Ralph had joked that too much pressure and they could explode. At least, Billie thought he was joking. What would happen if she cut the tyre? Would the air all rush out at once with a bang? She'd heard of people 'slashing car tyres' in radio plays but had never seen it done. On the radio, there was no bang, only a hissing noise as the air slowly escaped. Billie hoped they did good research for the plays. She was about to do the most terrible thing.

If she wanted to stop Stone, she needed to stop him from leaving with the only evidence she had against him. But she felt guilty. Tyres were heavily rationed. Many cars were up on bricks, having donated their tyres to ambulances. Billie, her knife in her hand, circled the red car to find the most worn-looking one. If she was going to do this, it had better be now.

She put the blade to the rubber and pulled. It left a little line in the tread but otherwise did nothing. She tried again, harder this time. Stupid, pathetic, weak girl! Why couldn't she do anything right? Angrily, she took the knife and stabbed it into the side of the tyre. It went in to the hilt. No noise of air. Gently, she tried tugging on it. It seemed jammed. Like King Arthur, she put her foot on the side of the tyre and with both hands and her full body weight she yanked at her pocket knife. It came out like butter. She landed backwards on her bottom, her elbows and backside scuffed with gravel. A gentle hiss emanated from the tyre as it slowly deflated.

Stone was going nowhere.

Now all she had to do was steal his car key.

***

When she got back into the building, she heard yelling and ducked into the open door of the empty classroom as two men barrelled down the corridor.

'Ow!'

One shoved the other against the wall in the corridor, the opposite side of the wall that Billie had her back against.

'You don't want me to make trouble for you, Stone.' It was Cummings' plummy voice. 'You simply need to do what is asked of you. None of these extra-curricular activities.'

Billie held her breath. Did Cummings know? Was Stone in trouble?

'They weren't supposed to blow it up…' Stone gasped, as though he was still being held in place.

'I've told you again and again. Keep your nose out of trouble. I don't want to have to throw you out of the RAF for good. Which is well within my power.'

'It was that kid, Dumbo. She tried to frame me…'

Cummings moved closer. 'You were seen running towards the explosion, trying to stop it.'

Yes, thought Billie. Explain that.

'I thought they were too close to other aircraft. I thought they'd damage them.'

Cummings sneered. 'You expect anyone to believe that?'

'So what if they don't? I hate the ATA. I want to come back *now*. I'm fed up of being a delivery boy.'

'Patience. You just have to wait. And making me cross trying to scramble your way back isn't going to work.'

'I'm ready for a bigger job.'

'Not until I know I can trust you.'

Billie didn't understand. Did Cummings believe him? He hadn't even lied properly!

'You can count on me, Wingco. You always can count on me.'

'Try and stay out of trouble and I'll smooth this over with Commander Wills.'

'They haven't got anything on me,' Stone said.

'It wasn't your bag?'

'Of course not! It was an American pilot called Bamford. She can take the rap.'

'Pity. I liked her.'

They moved on, in different directions.

Billie stood with her back pressed against the wall in fury. Stone had fooled Cummings as well as Pauline Gower. Billie sank to the floor. They were going to blame Nancy for the bag.

She wasn't sure what trouble Nancy would be in but she did know it wouldn't be good.

CHAPTER THIRTY-FIVE

'Pauline told her to come in the morning with her things. They are going to dismiss her,' said Jackie. 'I can't believe Nancy has done this; it makes no sense to me. She's honest to a fault.'

'She obviously isn't a smuggler,' Billie agreed.

'It was all top-end black market stuff. The stockings were nylons from America. Had a gold watch in there too, that was what was ticking. They've summoned her here tomorrow.'

'But why didn't they dismiss her right away? Is there still hope?'

'Stone,' Jackie said. 'He's in the briefing room right now, trying to convince Pauline and Commander Wills that they could trust her to come tomorrow and the police could be called then.'

'Stone was trying to stop her being arrested?' Billie didn't think that made any sense. He was, after all, the guilty party. She was certain of it.

'He was backed up by Cummings.'

Ah, thought Billie. He obviously wanted to make himself look innocent to Cummings. It would look suspicious if he were the only pilot to accuse Nancy when the rest of the officers couldn't believe it.

This was good, Billie thought. She had time to try and get his key and recover the list he had made. That would prove he was the person trying to smuggle the clothes and so prove Nancy was innocent. That was, if it still was tucked in that magazine.

'What will happen to Nancy?'

'She won't fly for the ATA again, that's for certain. If they arrest her and she's found guilty she'll either be deported or sent to prison.'

Bill's heart started to thump harder than ever.

She went back to the hangar and spent the rest of the afternoon working on the Liberator. Stone was there too and she watched him like a hawk. He seemed much more interested in this plane than any other. Even asking Ralph if he wanted him to test fly her.

'Tomorrow perhaps. It's getting dark already,' Ralph said. 'Besides, you need a co-pilot to fly this thing. Gribble might volunteer.'

'Why would I need a co-pilot?' Stone asked churlishly.

'She's four engines,' Ralph said slowly. 'You need at the very least a flight engineer.'

'American planes need more crew as a rule,' Billie said calmly, recalling the flight manuals that she had been reading in the mess. 'The B25 Mitchell is only two engines and the controls are so heavy you need someone else to even up the revs, boost on the boost levers or put down the wheels or flaps.'

'Shut up, Dumbo, the most you've ever flown is a Tiger Moth.'

'She's right. The American planes are hard on the arms,' Ralph said. 'The only thing that could fly this alone is an octopus with an extra eye for navigation.'

'Tomorrow then,' Stone said, relenting. 'We'll take her up with Gribble.'

He and Ralph shook on it and Ralph went to pack away his equipment and yell at Tommy for over-tightening various bolts. Billie kept a close eye on Stone. His car keys were in the front pocket of his trousers. She had to be patient.

She followed him back to the mess and, when he went out to report to ops, instead of following him and raising suspicion, she went to the main entrance, keeping an eye on his car, now one of the few vehicles left in the drive.

'Why haven't you gone home?' Stone's voice was right up behind her.

She whipped round. He had his parachute bag over his shoulder and his overnight bag. He was about to leave.

'I'll get the door for you,' she said politely, and opened the heavy entrance door.

'Thanks,' he said looking confused as the young cadet followed him out into the cold evening air.

Billie watched as he opened the passenger door and began to rummage on the car seat. She could see the magazine flop onto the floor of the car as he unearthed his hip flask. Billie moved quickly to the driver's side of the car and said loudly.

'Oh goodness!'

'What is it?'

'You've a flat tyre.'

He left the passenger door open and walked round to the front of the car. At the same time, Billie went to the passenger door.

Stone swore loudly. Billie quickly picked up the old magazine and immediately stuffed it into the waistband of her trousers.

'Shall I see if Ralph is about? We can pump it up,' Billie said innocently, running around to the driver's side of the car.

'Some idiot has slashed it.'

'Who could have done that?'

Stone didn't say anything, but by the look on his face he knew who had caused his flat tyre. He made a lunge for Billie's arm and with her wrist firmly in his grip, he dragged her back into the building, leaving his parachute, overnight bag and hip flask by the car.

'Ow,' she said.

'Shut up!'

She considered yelling out for help. But she didn't want anyone else to know she had damaged his car tyres. She didn't want to hear him say it. He took her into the map room and, using the key that was left on the desk, he opened the stationery cupboard and locked her inside it.

'You can stay in there.'

She heard his footsteps grow fainter and the door banged shut.

CHAPTER THIRTY-SIX

At this point Billie had a good cry.

She felt entirely responsible for Nancy's pending arrest. If she hadn't lied about her age, she and Nancy would still be friends. Nancy wouldn't have gone to Hamble. Billie wouldn't have run out to meet her and she never would have seen the smuggled bag. If she hadn't been so convinced Stone was a spy, she would have realised that instead of an elaborate code, it was just a list of underwear. She also felt bad about herself. She had ruined his car tyre, all because she had had a hard time explaining herself to Pauline Gower. If she'd confided in an adult from the start, she would never have got into the ATA in the first place. She should have told everyone she'd seen Stone's Spitfire crash and they'd have chucked him out for falsifying his accident report. She would never have joined up, and everyone would be better off without her.

A small voice in her head whispered, 'But Susan would be dead if you hadn't borrowed those eggs.'

Another joined it. 'And maybe Gribble would have hit the Liberator without you there.'

And another. 'And if you hadn't spoken to the First Lady, Tommy wouldn't have got flying lessons.'

Finally, a booming swell of emotion – it was an emotion rather than words – filled her head and she stopped crying. If it had spoken it would have said, 'You like flying, you silly girl. You belong in this place. Prove it.'

She opened her eyes. At first, she thought it was completely dark but as she became accustomed to the dimness, she realised there was a faint glow coming in through the gap at the bottom of the cupboard door.

She tried the handle but it was locked. She put her eye to the keyhole but the view was blocked by the key locking her inside. She began banging on the door. Yelling for help.

She couldn't hear anything. She dropped to the floor and peeked under the door. The room was lit by a desk lamp, but Stone wasn't there.

She'd be stuck overnight unless she could get out. She couldn't see in the cupboard but felt about in the darkness. A great many pens clattered to the floor, several rolling under the gap in the door. When she picked them up, she dislodged some yard-long rulers that had been propped up against the shelves. The noise of them hitting the cold tiled floor was incredible.

She opened up little boxes, stabbing her fingers on drawing pins which she carefully put back. She'd found some paperclips and thought for a moment of how she had heard of people able to pick locks.

She unravelled the paperclip and stuck it in the lock. The only thing that happened was the key moved a little back. That's when it occurred to her. She felt around the cupboard for some maps. She opened one up to make a large sheet and slid it under the door. She was going to use it to catch the key, which she would poke through the lock. Once it was on the map, she would slide it back to her side of the door and unlock it.

She gently pushed the key out of the lock. She heard it ring as it hit the floor. It bounced. Billie immediately peeked back under the door to see where it had landed. It had come to rest two inches from the edge of the paper.

She tried to slide the paper underneath it by pushing the map but this only moved it further away.

She had another go at picking the lock, which now was clear of the key, but she had no idea what she was doing. It didn't work and after a few minutes she sat back down against the shelves, defeated.

It was her sudden movement that dislodged the yard rulers again and they toppled over onto her.

'Ow!' She yelled at them and then realised something.

Again, she looked under the door. The key seemed impossibly far away, but she slid both yard rulers through the gap and…

'Yes!'

She could reach the key with them. She had to be really careful not to push it further away.

She used one ruler in to tap the key, so the other could more easily reach it. Then, oh so gently, she brought the two together. They were 'holding' the key between them. She had a flash of her mother with greasy hands, attempting to open the front door with her wrists to let Susan out of the house.

She inched the rulers towards her. The key paused on the lip of the paper. One tug and it made it over. She immediately slid the map with the rulers and key under the door.

Fumbling, she pushed the key in the lock. It opened. She was free! She emerged blinking into the dimly lit map room.

CHAPTER THIRTY-SEVEN

Billie jumped. She hadn't even checked! She pulled the crumpled magazine out of her waistband. She flicked through it and there, tucked in the pages, crinkled, was the note she had copied out. A list of smuggled underwear. She carefully folded it and placed it in her pocket. She had proof. That's when she heard an unmistakeable noise. It was an aeroplane engine starting up. Then another. Then another...

Immediately, Billie realised what was happening. Stone was going to steal the Liberator!

She flung herself out of the map room, leaving behind the mess of maps, rulers, paperclips and pens, and ran down the corridor towards the entrance onto the runway. There was the Liberator. No sign of the ARP wardens. No Home Guard either. Where were they?

The Liberator was out of the hangar and taxiing up the runway. Billie ran as fast as she could, falling over the grass verge in the darkness. She could hear the supercharger whine. The headlights were out, presumably to avoid strain on the batteries during the run-up. There was no way a plane this large could take off in secret.

She sprinted towards the plane, not daring to believe she'd get there in time. Her lungs were screaming as she crossed behind the plane. It taxied into position and stopped at the end of the runway. Keeping back to stay out of the slip-stream because it could take off at any moment, she went round in a big circle to avoid passing in front of the pilot's gaze. She hoped that Stone would be too busy checking his instruments to look out of the starboard window.

Billie balled her fists, and made a dive for the nose-wheel opening. It was much easier wiggling in when she wasn't carrying Ralph's tea. It only took a few seconds to climb up onto the anti-icer tanks. Her heart was hammering as she realised what she had done. She was inside the plane.

The engines began to roar. The noise grew along with the smile on Billie's face. Soon they were batting down the runway. The four engines throbbed a resonating deep note. Riding just above the wheel, Billie watched the dark wet runway skim past impossibly fast a few feet away. Nothing was holding on to her, no parent clutching her hand. No straps or belts stopping her from falling. It was just her, and the machine. By feel alone Billie knew they were airborne. The wheel below was still spinning. Then it retracted sharply, and she pressed up against the walls so it didn't hit her. It flicked a fine spray as it slowed. The nose-wheel door shut with a click and the air stopped swirling around her. Billie couldn't believe it had all really happened.

She was in the crawl space under the flight deck. Above her was a gap where she could peek out at floor level at the pilot's feet. Carefully, Billie stood up, expecting to see Stone's black boots. To Billie's surprise, she saw a second set of boots. Stone had a flight engineer with him. The droning of the engines made it impossible to hear what was being said. By bending down a little it was possible to study them up to the neck but beyond that it did not seem wise to investigate. Billie knew that if you looked at a person's face it inevitably drew their eyes to you. She couldn't work out who the co-pilot was. He was wearing a large black coat that covered his clothes. His shoes were no different to Stone's. A burning curiosity pulsed through Billie.

Billie heard a noise which she assumed was them switching onto the automatic pilot – a Sperry. It was remarkably smooth. The engines hummed like a lullaby. Billie was too excited to feel sleepy, but it would have been nice to relax. She tried to sit on the shelf but was afraid of falling asleep and rolling onto the nose-wheel doors. If she did that, she would fall out when they were opened. Standing up she could rest her arms on the cross-beam supporting the floor of the flight deck. She did doze off every now and then, only to wake up with a start when she began to sag in the knees. The blue instrument panel lights were on now and she wondered if Stone, too, was having forty winks.

To make matters worse, the cabin heater was turned on. This was right in front of her and burned the petrol vapour from the blower section of the engine. The fumes made Billie incredibly thirsty and light-headed. She desperately wanted a cup of tea. She took her red woollen hat off and unbuttoned her coat.

After a long spell of standing in the dark, the popping in Bill's ears let her know they were descending. It was noticeable too when Stone took over the controls again. The plane lurched and bounced, and Billie made sure she had a good grip on the beam. When the doors re-opened it was still dark and down below was a glint of moonlight reflecting off a stretch of water. Billie thought of all the sharks and U-boats that she could soon be swimming with. They circled and Billie saw a darker spot. Land. She couldn't tell where they were, but she knew they must have been flying for a couple of hours. A Liberator, with four engines, could go anywhere in that time: Ireland, occupied France. Even Germany? The plane came over the sea again and then swooped in to land. After a bit of taxiing the engines stopped.

'Made it,' said Stone.

The mystery flight engineer stood up and walked out of Billie's sight. Billie didn't know if she should try to get out. She didn't want to lose sight of Stone but she didn't know who was outside, in the middle of the night. She could hear footsteps and an engine. No one was talking. The decision was made for her as the plane was towed off.

Billie was frustrated. In her fear of not being caught she had let Stone get away. Still, there were no sounds of other aircraft. Wherever he was, he hadn't flown off. She knew that the ground crew would have to do the post-flight checks. She decided to wait until the engines were being run for oil dilution. No one could be working on the outside of the ship while the propellers were turning.

Billie dropped down onto the concrete and stayed beside the wheel. She was in an enormous hangar. She quickly stepped out and decided the best thing to do was to march purposefully in one direction as if she knew exactly where she was going and what she was doing. The chill was astounding. She buttoned her coat back up and jammed her hat over her head. There was no one in sight so Billie just headed for the next ship up the line. It was a Mosquito, a twin-engined light bomber. Only this one wasn't in RAF colours. It was painted to look like BOAC, a civilian airline. As she got closer, she saw its bomb bay door hatch was open. Inside were crates.

She thought it strange and was about to get closer when a voice behind her called, 'Hey.' There was a mechanic following her inquiringly.

'You looking for someone?'

The relief Billie felt at hearing a Scottish accent must have shown on her face. She was still in Britain. She didn't say anything, just beamed at him.

The mechanic looked tired. 'Did you come over on that ship?'

Billie said nonchalantly, 'That's right. The Liberator.'

'The crew are with security,' he said. 'Come on, I'll take you.'

Billie couldn't think of a reason not to follow him.

'You're a civilian?' he asked.

'ATA cadet,' she replied, trying to keep up with his fast pace.

'That explains why you're a lassie,' he said.

'Why was that Mosquito kitted out like an Anson? They're bombers, not transport planes.'

'You should nae have seen that. Keep schtum about it.'

Billie didn't want to ask where she was because that would really raise suspicions. Every crew member should know where they are and where they are going. He didn't ask any more questions but took her into a rather flimsy-looking office building. They climbed up metal steps which had small icicles hanging from them.

Blinking in the sudden brightness, it took Billie a moment to work out that she was in a large office. Behind the desk was a man in a dressing gown with a scarf around his neck. He looked more worried than angry. Next to him was a man in overalls, and a sleepy-looking young man in an RAF pilots' uniform that was buttoned up wrong.

Opposite them, sitting by a small heater, was an apprehensive-looking Stone. And... Billie couldn't believe it. A man sat next to Stone, stroking his moustache.

'Cummings!' she exclaimed.

All heads turned to face her.

'What's this?' said the man behind the desk.

'She says she's ATA,' said the mechanic.

'A stowaway!' Cummings laughed.

Stone looked like someone had just smacked him on the bottom. 'How the hell did you get here?'

'They stole the Liberator!' Billie said quickly. 'You have to tell White Waltham.'

'This is Billie Swift,' Stone said. 'She was accused of selling underwear on the black market and has evidently stowed away in the plane that we requisitioned to get away from the authorities.'

'Telephone White Waltham,' Billie said confidently. 'They'll prove he's lying.'

'Telephone them in the morning,' Cummings said coolly. 'They aren't military. There won't be anyone there until when? 8am?'

The man in the dressing gown looked bewildered. 'I'm really not comfortable with all this.'

'Where is Reynolds?' Cummings asked. 'He'd sort this out in no time.'

'Away. Back tomorrow.' The man looked more worried. 'This really is improper. Why don't you have the correct paperwork?'

'I thought we did,' Cummings said simply, shrugging. 'It must have got muddled somewhere.'

'You put me in a very difficult position. As a fellow wing commander, I vote we wait for Group Commander Reynolds to arrive back tomorrow and we can sort it all out. In the meantime, I'd better find you bunks in the barracks to sleep.'

'Don't be silly, Wingco,' Cummings said in a relaxed voice. 'You shouldn't give us special treatment just because we share a uniform.'

'Sure he can!' Stone spluttered.

Cummings ignored him. 'While we all know there has been a miscommunication somewhere, I admit that on the surface it looks like Stone and I have stolen a military asset. You have to put us under lock and key until the mess can be cleared up in the morning.'

The man in the dressing gown nodded. 'That's very understanding of you.'

'Not at all. It is what I would do.'

'And the girl?'

'I'm sure she'll be comfortable with us; she is tougher than most.'

'This is an airbase; we don't have prisoner cells...'

'Pop us in an air raid shelter. They've only got one door. It will only be for a few hours,' Cummings said jovially.

'Very well,' said the man behind the desk. 'Let's all try and get some rest before morning.'

Billie looked flabbergasted at the man behind the desk. 'You're not serious?'

'If they murder you, I promise to add it to their list of charges.'

Somehow Billie didn't feel overly reassured.

CHAPTER THIRTY-EIGHT

The air raid shelter was comfortable. Billie had her own bunk, a blanket and more importantly, cold cheese and lentil savouries and a flask of tea. It wasn't so much that they were tasty but there were four of them. Each.

'You eat like a dog,' Stone said.

Billie wolfed down another savoury and shrugged. She couldn't work out why Cummings was looking so happy. Stone hadn't touched his food. He was pacing up and down in the semi-darkness. Billie decided to lie down, she was tired.

It was a few minutes later she heard Stone's voice whispering.

'We're going to be put in prison.'

'We won't. It's all part of the plan.'

'How can being locked in here be part of your plan?' Stone paused and looked at Billie.

'Even if she is listening, I promise there is nothing she can do,' Cummings said confidently. 'We're going to fly that Mosquito out of here.'

'Steal a Mosquito? Why? Isn't it under guard? I'm not getting shot at.'

'We aren't going to get shot. I'm hoping they will give it to us.'

'Give it to us?' Stone echoed, disbelieving.

'Oh, they will beg us to take it. Besides, if I'm the highest-ranking officer on site, I can place the order myself.'

'But you're not. That other wing commander locked us in here.'

'He won't be a problem much longer.' Billie opened an eye and saw his moustache curl. 'I sent another message.'

'To who?' Stone asked.

'To whom.' Cummings corrected him as though he were Stone's father. 'The Luftwaffe of course. Our exact location, height of radar, the lot. They'll send a plane or two. As soon as there is enough light, they will bomb the target.'

Billie shut her eyes before she was caught eavesdropping. Cummings had been in touch with the enemy? If they bombed the barracks, and came in too low for radar, wouldn't that mean there would be no warning? It would get everyone who wasn't in a bomb shelter killed!

It was clear this news had shocked Stone too.

'Target? You mean the wing commander in the pilots' barracks? Now wait a minute! You said it was a big job. But you're talking about murder... dammit, it is treason!'

'You had no objection when I ordered that Messerschmitt back in October. You remember, when the First Lady was at White Waltham?'

Stone was obviously trying to remember the events of Billie's first day at the airfield. 'I thought we'd got lucky. You said you were going to set off the air raid sirens so I could pick up a bag from you. You didn't say you were going to start a real air raid!'

'I had to make it believable,' Cummings reasoned. 'If those damned pilots would have stayed in the shelter, we could have swapped bags and no one would have been the wiser.'

'You've got to call it off, Wingco! They could kill everyone! *And* they'll destroy the Mosquito.'

'Not to worry.' Cummings smiled. 'I gave them precise instructions to leave that hangar unharmed.'

'Weren't you stationed here for a time?' Stone said. 'You're willing to let chaps you fought alongside get blitzed?'

'The pilots here aren't like us, Stone. This place was full of wanna-be heroes. They know nothing of sacrifice. They never go toe-to-toe. All they do is bomb ships and fish the Jerries out of the sea.' Cummings' voice was persuasive and cool. 'Besides, the men flying that Mosquito to Sweden are Norwegian civilians in BOAC uniforms.'

'A bomb can't tell the differences in nationality! Our boys will snuff it with them. We should warn them,' Stone said.

'No! If we are the only pilots to survive, then it will be up to us to fly the Mosquito to Sweden with the gold.'

Gold? Cummings had gone mad. Why would the Mosquito have gold in it? Luckily, Stone asked the question that was screaming inside Billie's mind.

'I don't understand. Why are they sending gold to Sweden?'

'To buy ball bearings. It is a choke point in the war economy. Everyone needs ball bearings and the Swedes manufacture the most. If the British cut off the Nazis' supply, the Germans will flounder. So they are going to try to buy the lot by sneaking a plane-load of ingots and gold sovereigns over the North Sea. Never mind knickers and nylons, this is real money! When we take that plane, we'll be millionaires!'

So that was why the Mosquito was painted with civilian markings, thought Billie. You couldn't fly military aircraft over neutral airspace. It was a clever plan. Mosquitoes were the fastest plane. Once airborne nothing could catch them, so they didn't need to be armed. Billie was revolted by Cummings. To steal the plane just for the gold, when he knew it was important for the war effort. And to tell the enemy classified information. He was evil and Stone was working for him! What would they do with her? She knew everything now. Would they kidnap her or... worse?

Strangely it wasn't her companions Billie was most fearful of. It was the upcoming Luftwaffe strike. Soon she would hear the dreadful sound of enemy aircraft and feel the ground vibrate with explosions. She felt sick. She looked at the bunker and wondered if it were strong enough should they receive a direct hit.

Stone also seemed nervous. His voice sounded strangled as he realised what he had got himself into.

'Listen, Wingco... I'm not sure about this. This isn't what I thought you meant by a "big job".'

'The number of times I've saved you,' Cummings snarled. 'Bailing you out because you make rookie errors. Running out of fuel in that Spitfire full of black-market whiskey... and for some daft reason setting light to it!'

'I didn't want the whiskey to be discovered. I had to think on my feet.'

'So what you wanted discovered was an upside-down Spitfire with no fuel in the tanks in burnt out field full of charred glass bottles? How do you think that would have looked if I hadn't come to the rescue?'

'I said I was sorry.'

'I had to pay that mad gamekeeper off, and the farmer to help move the plane. That money is coming out of your cut of the gold.'

Stone was silent. He paced over to a bunk and lay down on it. Billie watched him until he turned out the lamp. Now all she could do was ait.

CHAPTER THIRTY-NINE

Billie was wide awake. The only sound she could hear was Cummings' deep snores. Each one sounded like a distant plane.

In the darkness she heard movement. Stone was getting out of bed. His feet plodded past her head as he made his way to the exit. She could hear him climbing up the steps to the door. It was shut, of course. Bolted at the top from the outside. They were prisoners.

She sat up and listened. Cummings was still asleep. Suddenly she heard a metallic screech and a faint, deep booming noise. She reached for her shoes. She scuttled after Stone, her fingertips stretching into the dark. Once she reached the steps, she took them two at a time to see that Stone had lifted the metal door off its hinges. He'd laid it down in the frozen grass.

It still felt like night time. Billie scanned the horizon for Stone. To the east, the stars gave way to a sinister red glow. It was still a while before sunrise. She spotted the shadow of Stone trotting back towards the hangars. She ran to keep up.

'Go away, Dumbo.'

'Where are you going?'

'I'm getting out of here. I don't want anything to do with it.'

Billie was about to argue that they needed to go back and warn the base right away, when she heard it. There was a faint grumbling of an engine.

Stone swore. They both stopped. Where to run? Take cover in the hangar?

'No, no, no!' Stone cried.

Somewhere above the wide stretch of black sea, a faint dark spot appeared though the mist. It was coming closer.

'We need to warn everyone!' Billie said.

As she spoke, she heard ack-ack fire. It sounded measly. Just one gun. The plane returned fire with a surgeon's precision. Their ack-ack fell silent. Then the plane fired again, presumably taking out another defence that hadn't even spotted it yet. The plane knew exactly where to shoot. Cummings had told them.

'Get back to the bunker! Run!' Stone gasped.

They didn't make it to the bunker. As they ran back, the plane was overhead. Stone grabbed Billie and shoved her into the grass verge. The frosty grass crunched beneath them and she turned her head to watch the plane roar past. Her eyes were accustomed to the half-darkness now and she could make out its familiar details.

Billie held her breath as the Heinkel 111 banked sharply. Its bomb bay door yawned open and just before Billie screwed up her eyes, she saw the tiny pill-shaped silhouettes tip out.

Bright explosions flashed through her eyelids. Stone hugged her as the ground shook beneath them. Blast after blast echoed around them. Soil erupted; masonry cascaded from every direction. The barracks buildings had taken a direct hit... someone, somewhere had started a siren.

Billie heard the plane's gurgle fade. She looked for it.

'He's going to come round again,' she said. Her voice sounding strangely distant after all the explosions.

'Don't be daft...' Stone began but he looked confused as the plane indeed seemed to circle.

Stone quickly got up, his hand grabbing her wrist and, unlike her reluctance when he had dragged her to the cupboard, she sprinted with him back to the bunker.

Jumping down the steps, he yelled for Cummings.

But Cummings had gone. Evidently, hadn't realised the danger wasn't over. It was, after all, unheard of for a plane to unload its bombs and then come back again. It was opening itself up to counter attack.

Both Billie and Stone climbed back up the steps and peaked out. The siren was deafening, masking the Heinkel's grunting engines. Once again, it was a dark silhouette against the blood red daybreak, coming in for a second sweep. Had anyone had time to get to the guns?

It happened in slow motion. Billie could see the few people who had survived the first wave of destruction running to various points. Some pilots, still in their nightclothes, were limping to the planes... attempting to scramble into the Spitfires that were lined up on the grass. Someone else had started a truck and was driving it over to the flattened barracks. Everyone was running past the hangar except one figure, Cummings, greedily running into it. He was inside, looking up at the Mosquito when it happened.

The Heinkel opened its guns and sprayed everyone on the grass with bullets. It hit nearly all the aircraft. Billie was thankful she couldn't hear the screams of the people over the siren but she did hear something. It was

Stone. He made the sound of a frightened animal and then Billie saw: the Heinkel dropped its second load of bombs.

Evidently, the Luftwaffe hadn't taken Cummings's instructions about only hitting the barracks to heart. They didn't care about the gold or the Mosquito. They only cared about one thing. Death.

The hangar suffered a direct hit. Aghast, Billie watched as the whole thing wobbled and then the entire wall blew outwards. The people who had taken shelter there from the gunfire were crushed. The roof hung in the air for a moment above the Liberator, the Mosquito and Cummings before it slammed down on top of them. The Heinkel took a few extra pot shots with its rear guns, hitting the fire truck and destroying a Hurricane before finally turning and making its escape.

CHAPTER FORTY

The airfield was burning. The sirens wailed. A single anti-aircraft cannon finally started to fire. Far too late. Billie was so shaken she didn't even want to cry.

Stone had started off again. He was jogging towards the smouldering control tower, one of the few buildings not to have received a direct hit. All of its windows were smashed through from the shockwaves. Billie jumped over what remained of some picnic benches that had been blown fifty feet from what had been a gathering place for ground crew. Two ARP wardens rushed past them, both of their faces blank with shock as they bravely charged towards the destruction. Billie knew they had no hope of coping with the fires that were starting to bloom out of the rubble. Stone ran into the main building.

A lone woman in a WAAF uniform was running up the stairs.

'Hey wait!' he yelled.

'I've instructions,' the WAAF yelled back, carrying on up the stairs.

They followed her into the control tower. She was spookily calm despite having her hair still in rollers and shattered glass covering everything.

'Radio and telephone lines are out, sir. Power lines too.'

'Coast's clear,' Stone said, looking through the blasted windows. 'Are there any more coming?'

'Yes sir,' the woman said. 'Our last communications were a formation of enemy planes about twenty minutes out.'

'Why no siren?'

'Command assured us they weren't heading for us... but no one saw that bomber. It must have come in under the radar.'

'Did you get word out that we're under attack?'

'I don't know if my communications got through,' she said. 'The first hit was the radio tower by the barracks. Talk about luck!'

Billie knew it wasn't luck. Cummings had told it exactly when and where to bomb and how to get around the radar. He wanted to be the only option to fly the Mosquito.

'Fighter Command could still be in the dark!' Stone shook his head.

'I've just been to the dovecote and have sent a pigeon. Winkie. She's our best. I told Charlotte... sorry, Company Assistant Hawkins, to cycle into town and see if any of their lines are working.'

Billie knew they really were in trouble if their survival depended on a pigeon and a bicycle.

'I'll go up and radio them from a plane,' Stone said. 'If I fly south, I'll get nearer to intact radio towers.'

'What plane?' she said as dawn revealed the devastation of the airfield.

'There are a couple of Spits in one piece over there,' Stone said. 'The girl and I will take them.'

The woman didn't protest at the idea of Billie flying.

'One is a camera plane. No guns. Don't go bumping into the enemy.'

'I suggest you either go and help get people out of the rubble or get some shelter.'

'Good luck.'

They left the tower and jumped down the stairs.

'Alright, Dumbo,' Stone said. 'We're going to scramble. Do you know what echelon is?'

'A tight formation where the wingman sits to the side and back from the leader,' said Billie.

'That's it. We are going to take off, head a few miles out to sea, then turn south. That way we won't risk getting shot at by trigger-happy defences. I imagine they'll be a bit jumpy this morning.'

'We're going to take off? Now?'

'Unless you want a cup of tea and a crumpet first,' Stone said sarcastically. 'Come on, Dumbo, you've dreamt of this – solo flight in a Spit! Just focus on me, use your throttle to match my pace, keep your nose in line. Piece of cake.'

'I need a map...' Billie said.

'I locked you into a cupboard full of them and you didn't pinch one? Here,' Stone magically produced one from his coat pocket and handed it to her. He then reached around and dug out a pocket diary. On the inside cover there was a map of Britain. 'I'll use my little one.'

Billie didn't know what to think about having a leader using a map that was barely larger than his thumb, but she certainly didn't want to go without one herself.

Right now, she needed all the confidence she could get and clutched the OS map close to her chest.

They ran over to the Spitfires. One sparkled a little in the morning frost and seemed to smile at her. Stone was with a member of ground crew, sheltering under the green one's wing. The poor man had been hit with shrapnel and, despite being as pale as paper, still managed to help them find a parachute each from somewhere in the rubble of the building.

They could only find one helmet with radio attachments. That was probably for the best, Billie thought, as she had never learnt to use the radio with the ATA anyway.

Instead of a helmet, she kept on her red woollen hat. She tied the bobbles under her chin so it wouldn't get ripped off during take-off and would keep her ears warm.

'You look ridiculous,' Stone said.

'Yes,' Billie said. 'Which one do I fly?'

'You take the blue. It's a PV IV. It isn't armoured, so it should be easier to manoeuvre. Careful with her; she's got no cannon or guns so your only defence is to out-fly them.'

Billie nodded. She was nervous so didn't correct him. It was a PR not PV. PR stood for Photographic Reconnaissance.

'Dumbo,' Stone said as he strapped her in the cockpit. 'I didn't know he was... You... you know I didn't, right?'

Billie nodded. 'Do we have enough fuel to get to White Waltham?'

'The tanks should be full, ready to scramble. But I'll find us somewhere safe to land. Just stick by me. Remember, when we get somewhere, stay in the circuit and land after me, alright?'

She nodded.

'We best be quick. See you on the other side!'

Billie had sat in a Spitfire before now, mainly to pick out all the cigarette butts pilots had left in them. Being strapped in, and being shown the minor snags by a bleeding Scottish man who trembled a little as he cleaned her windshield was a whole different experience.

She could only see forward through a little triangle, as the nose and wings were in the way. Stone leant in and put up her cruising revs and boost to RAF settings, which were higher than ATA's fuel-saving settings. Billie would have preferred to be flying a bit slower but she had no choice but to do as Stone said.

Not only did they have to get a message to Fighter Command, but they had to get up in the air before the next lot of planes came over.

The sun still hadn't risen although the sky was brightening from deep red to orange, revealing the fog that swept in from over the bay. Billie kept searching the distance for signs of the enemy.

Her heart thumped. There, emerging out of the mist... She thought could see something. Maybe it was gulls.

It felt like a dream. She had no time to think but speedily ran through the system checks that she and Nancy did together in the Anson. Knowing the Spitfire was a more serious plane, she recalled Diana's warnings of a loose trim and set the rudder. Her fuel mixture was rich, her ailerons wiggled, her flaps waved.

Stone's engine had started.

'Check,' she yelled and the Merlin engine purred into life. It seemed so happy to be rescued.

'Hello,' she whispered. 'I'm Billie.'

It buzzed happily. Knowing how nose-heavy it was, she gently tapped the throttle on and off rather than risking braking. Stone was already on the runway. It was fortunately free of debris. She jittered over. The cold air blew into the cockpit, filling her nose with a mix of smoke, burning rubber and sea air. Stone was waiting for her at the end of the runway, his hand held up to show he was about to take off. As she pulled up behind him his hand dropped and his Spitfire thundered with noise. She powered the throttle and gasped as her chair whacked her in the back. The power was like nothing she had ever felt before. She was catching him. Never had she gone so fast in her life.

Stone's nose was gently rising. Seeing she'd also reached speed, she pulled back, what she thought was carefully. She shot vertically into the sky. She whooped. The plane was unbelievable. She pointed the nose back down, and swooped. It weaved and bobbed as she experimented with the controls.

Everywhere she pointed it, it went. She levelled off, held the controls with her knees and used both hands and all her strength to shut the hood. Once the canopy was closed, she tried to find Stone, somewhere beneath her. She spotted him just in time. Turning to look over her left shoulder she saw a swarm of Luftwaffe planes, flying in a casual formation like geese. Had they seen the Spitfires?

She came in close on Stone's tail, and sat behind his left wing. From here all she could do was focus on not losing him or crashing into him. He deliberately flew low, into the sea mist, making her job harder but presumably making it harder for an enemy plane to find them.

They had been flying for a few minutes, according to Billie's compass in a north-easterly direction. Billie could scarcely see anything below except, every now and then, a flash of churning sea. All the rest was just grey clouds and yellow muck. The light wasn't enough to map read by and besides, she couldn't do that and stay in formation at the same time, so she just kept hoping Stone would stick to the plan and stay on course.

By now the yellow muck had transformed into thick, grey cloud. It was so thick that Stone's Spitfire looked like a ghost, then a shadow. Then, without warning, it disappeared altogether. He wasn't there! Billie could see only thick cloud in all directions. If he was still there, she might accidentally crash into him at any moment. She stuck to the course, her head whipping round in search of his plane.

She was on her own.

CHAPTER FORTY-ONE

Billie had no idea where she was. She went down low to circle, only a few hundred yards above the ocean. It wasn't raining hard but the light drizzle made the visibility awful. She had never wanted the sun to rise faster in all her life. There was no point trying to pinpoint her position because there were no features – only dark churning water. She didn't dare stay in one place very long. She wondered if there were any German battleships sneaking around the coast. She certainly didn't feel like being shot down. She didn't consider finding her way back to the airfield; she'd be flying straight into enemy aircraft. Besides, if she overshot the airfield by just a few miles, she'd be in danger of crashing into the side of a Scottish mountain.

Flying in circles was no good. She came back up to just below the cloud and resumed her course. She needed to find the coast. If she kept this easterly course she would end up in Denmark. She needed to get back to England.

She looked at her map. Stone's original plan had been to travel out to sea to avoid the defences around the Firth of Forth and then turn south to fly over England. She turned sharply south. The clouds grew lower and lower. She should see the coast coming up on her right side. But she didn't. Her eyes kept playing tricks and the visibility was so bad she considered jettisoning the hood.

She decided it was best to throttle back to ATA cruising revs and boost. If she was lost, she needed to conserve fuel. Where was the coast? Then, as she noticed that daylight was breaking, Billie hit sea fog. Low sea fog. Right down on the water. She had no choice. She looked tearfully at the instruments in front of her, trying to remember all that she'd been taught and rammed open the throttle, pulled the control column back and zoomed steeply upwards. Inexpertly, Billie tried to keep the angle of climb constant. Suddenly, at five thousand feet, the clouds splintered into bright wintery sunshine. Beneath the little Spitfire, the white clouds stretched in all directions like a soft woollen blanket. They cast long shadows across each other as the large yellow sun peaked over the horizon. It was then that Billie noticed that the wings of her Spitfire were painted a beautiful azure blue. As she admired them, she saw an aircraft and immediately turned towards it, hoping it might be Stone. At once she saw it was just a twin-engined Dakota, going the wrong way.

Billie turned back, correcting her course. *Look down in mercy, hear our prayer, for those in peril in the air.*

Stop being dramatic. She was fine. Her plane was intact. She had fuel. She would find land. It would be OK.

She kept a close eye on the clock as well as the compass. After six and a half minutes she looked down as the white clouds turned yellow. Was it smog from a town? There was a little gap in the cloud, she could see the sea. No land, no houses… something was wrong. She was feeling properly scared now. ATA dictum as spoken by Gribble's serious voice echoed through her head.

'If in doubt bail out.'

Billie thought the best thing to do would be to make sure she was over land, then pray that whoever had packed this parachute knew what they were doing. But where was the land? If she bailed out over the water she could drown like Amy Johnson.

She continued on for another achingly slow three minutes. Still no land in the gaps between the clouds. She hadn't known the drift when Stone chose the course. It didn't matter where her Spitfire was pointing, the general wind speed and direction could mean she was miles further out to sea or barely any distance from the land.

What if she had travelled out to sea further east than the coast of Norfolk? If that were so, if she continued to fly south, the first land she would see would be Nazi-occupied Belgium... That is, if she had enough petrol to get her there.

She had had two full tanks of fuel when she left, but she had wasted some, circling like an idiot. She needed to find the coast. England must be somewhere west. She decided to change course. Once she found it, she could calm down, work out where she was and use her map and compass to find a way to get home. Seeing another gap in the clouds she dived for it, hoping that land would be visible from underneath.

For several minutes she saw nothing at all, then the wash of a large boat showed up white through the gloom. She was now at two hundred feet: dangerously low. The waves rose up, seeming like they might lick the bottom of her aircraft. Only here was the cloud thin enough for her to see more clearly. She could just make out a little sheen of light ahead, a thin line of white in the yellow.

Billie peered at it anxiously. Land at last? Cliffs? It obviously was not the White Cliffs of Dover, she thought to herself and, as she got closer, she realised it was a north to south line of perfect white sandy beach. Whooping, she turned to follow it and there, right beside her on the left-hand side of her plane, were the huge rocks of the Farne Islands. She had her finger right by them on her map. God couldn't have made a better signal for her than writing YOU ARE HERE in the sky.

She chuckled as she zoomed past them. How easy it would have been to smash into them in the low visibility. She loved them; they had saved her.

She kept close to the coast, making sure to conserve fuel. She flew low over the water, threading her plane between Croquet Island and the coast and buzzing low over the sleepy fishing towns who were only just waking up. She rose higher when she went past Whitley Bay and South Shields, fearful of being used for target practice.

She had a plan. She'd creep along the coast as far as Hartlepool then, hoping not to come across too many balloon obstructions or trigger-happy ack-ack boys, she would circle Middlesbrough and head straight south. From there she would fly directly over number seven ferry pool near Leeds. She knew what the airfield looked like, having travelled there a couple of times with Nancy in the Anson. Once there, she could send a message to White Waltham explaining what had happened and another message to Fighter Command if it wasn't too late.

The fog lifted, and although she saw some balloons in the distance, she managed to stick to her plan. She flew just below the cloud line, staying clear of the North Yorkshire Moors on her left. It was at this point she noticed a shadow overhead.

Looking up she saw the underside of another aeroplane. Luckily it wasn't a German fighter but a Hawker Hurricane. Then a second Hurricane slipped in beside her, wing tip to wing tip. What where they doing? Billie thought it best to keep her Spitfire as straight and level as possible as the one overhead dropped down, then back a bit to take a position by her tail. She felt rather squashed. They were flying a lot closer than she had to Stone, and she was terrified of bumping into them. If these pilots knew this was her first ever solo flight, Billie doubted they would have kept their formation so confidently tight.

They were obviously having great fun. The plane to her rear opened his throttle and parked next to her other wing. They flew either side of her, so she could look at them. They were roaring with laughter.

There was little doubt they could tell that she wasn't a man, as Billie hadn't done her hair up and it spilled down below her childish bobble hat. They pointed with glee at her hat, clapping in delight. One pilot put his arm on his chest, the other as far out as he could and mimed dancing a waltz. The moron had his eyes shut in romantic bliss. Boys were really stupid.

Billie had no way of telling them to go away other than to gesture 'shoo' at them with her free hand. This only seemed to encourage them. Billie realised she had missed number seven ferry pool near Leeds and was praying they would leave her before she was made to fly further off course.

Eventually, they stopped mucking about and gave her the thumbs up. She returned the gesture and they peeled off, heading back north.

CHAPTER FORTY-TWO

Billie considered turning and trying to find the airbase to attempt a landing. She wasn't confident she would be able to find it; none of this countryside was familiar. She was entrusting her current location to the thin railway line that was just about visible by the thick trees and hedgerows. But she realised, if she did land this far north, she likely wouldn't make it back to White Waltham until tomorrow. She'd have to take the train and by then, Nancy would be dismissed or even arrested.

The fuel gauge was drooping. The larger of the two tanks was nearly empty. She held her breath and switched tanks. The great Merlin engine gave a little splutter but droned on as before. She breathed out and looked out the window.

She was still flying south, just under the clouds. The visibility had improved but she could spot heavy bands of rain in the distance to her right.

Looking down at the fields below Billie's heart skipped a beat. It was the river Trent. She was sure of it. She put her face up against the curved Perspex sides of the Spitfire to peer forwards. It was still hard to identify over the large engine cowling. She wiggled the ailerons this way and that to look out of the side of the cockpit at the dark river, winding a familiar shape through the fields. Billie was so eager to see more she accidentally pushed the Spitfire too far and promptly got stuck upside down.

She remembered Diana's tale about the powder compact falling out of her top pocket and into the bubble canopy when she had first attempted a barrel roll. But she didn't remember how Diana had righted herself.

Still, while upside down with a face full of dust, hair, and flakes of Scottish mud, she snatched her map and studied the countryside. There, in the distance she saw the familiar fields that surrounded the Ratcliffe airfield at number six ferry pool. She could land there…

Another thought trickled into Billie's mind. She had done the journey from Leicester to White Waltham at least twice a week for the last few months in the Anson with Nancy. She knew it so well. The thought of her running into ops and shoving the underwear list under Pauline Gower's nose made her heart beat faster. She could prove the black-market pants smuggler was Stone, not Nancy! It was too important not to try for.

She tried to do the maths in her head. She reasoned she had about thirty minutes of fuel left in the tank. Thirty times sixty. Three sixes are eighteen. Add two noughts. That's it, one thousand eight hundred seconds before she ran out of fuel and wrecked the aeroplane. Loads of time.

Blood pounded in Billie's ears as the Spitfire shot further south, still upside down. The familiar Northamptonshire countryside sped past her head.

The cruising air speed of the Anson was around one hundred and twenty miles per hour. It usually took Nancy fifty minutes to fly from Ratcliffe to White Waltham. Billie was going at two hundred and ten miles an hour, which she thought was the correct speed to conserve fuel.

She needed to work out how far it was between Ratcliffe and White Waltham, then work out if she had enough fuel to get her there... distance is time multiplied by speed. Nancy was going at one hundred and twenty-five miles an hour for fifty minutes... how far did the Anson fly?

'Flying is an art not a science.'

A cold sweat trickled downwards, up her back. Billie exhaled and swung the plane this way, then that. She flipped the Spitfire back the right way. The plane immediately carried on in its barrel roll and flipped back upside down. She swore and remembered what Nancy had said about the artificial horizon. Focusing on the line this time, and ignoring the planet swinging around her head, she held her breath and flipped over again. This time she adjusted in time and the blue Spitfire calmed itself into a steady cruise.

She adjusted her course, heading as Nancy would for the ferry pool at Thame. Once there, she would bank to avoid the Chiltern Hills, thread through the Goring Gap and follow the railway line to White Waltham.

She was fudging the maths like Stone did in class. She reasoned that if it took an Anson fifty minutes, it should take a Spitfire just over half that time. Which was exactly thirty minutes. 'Besides,' she imagined Stone saying, 'the headwind is never the same, nor is the drift. You've got to roll the dice. That's flying.'

There was a headwind. That meant she would be using more fuel than normal. It was going to be close.

She tried to forget that Stone's crash which she had witnessed had been caused by him running out of fuel.

She watched as Thame came into view. If she were sensible, she could land here. It would be what Gribble would do. It's what Nancy would do. What would Stone do?

She turned west, keeping a look out for the Goring Gap. Gentle rolling English meadows zipped beneath her. They were coated in a white mist that made the trees and buildings stand black against them. It wasn't too thick; she could still spot the Thames and turned sharply south, following it closely between the hills. She saw the railway line join it. Her tank registered empty. If she got lost now, she would be done for.

The smoke of Reading lay ahead and she rose higher, fearful of, not the barrage balloons themselves, but the invisible wires that could slice right through her. Soaring upwards she allowed herself to giggle again. The Spitfire seemed to know where she wanted to go before she did. Once clear of the town she banked, putting the plane into a spin as she came closer to the ground, confident of its ability to quickly correct as she scooped its nose up and began to look out for the familiar church tower.

She had nearly made it. She joined the White Waltham circuit. The familiar airfield, the church, the railway line. The pub on the far corner. Her school, the post office, and her house, the back yard full of chickens and... oh. She'd seen something. Only for a moment. But now was not the time to think about chickens. She had to be quick.

She needed two hands to pull up the lever for the landing gear. It didn't clunk as nicely as the Anson but at least she didn't have to winch it by hand. This time she managed to open the hood with one arm. Wind whipped around the cockpit as she turned again into the breeze. Slowing the Spitfire right down, and still with an eye out for queue-barging Liberators, she brought the Spitfire in line with the runway and made her descent. She wanted so much to get this right. Seventy miles an hour. Gently does it, you've plenty of runway... the ground came up like an old friend to meet her. One touch, no bounce. It was what Diana would call, 'a daisy cutter of a landing'.

CHAPTER FORTY-THREE

If she had hoped Ralph would be surprised to see her, she wasn't disappointed. He couldn't have looked more shocked if Hitler himself had been flying the plane. Her red hat made her instantly recognisable.

'Turn her off, turn her off!' he said, overcome with amazement. 'Billie!'

She undid her straps, patting the airplane. Her knee gave way as she tried to jump out. She hadn't realised how overcome she was.

'Steady.' He jumped up on the wing and offered a hand.

'Did you see my landing?' Billie asked.

He laughed. 'Have you come down from Heaven?'

The doors of the main building opened and Pauline Gower came running out, followed by Diana, Fairweather, Chile, Gribble and Tommy.

'You're alive!' yelled Tommy.

Pauline ran straight up to her and the moment Billie jumped down off the wing she was immediately picked up.

'Oh you stupid, brilliant, idiotic child!' she exclaimed, as she squeezed Billie so hard that she thought her ribs would break.

Fairweather's large hand patted her on the shoulder as he said, 'Strange-looking Liberator you brought home.'

'Where's Nancy?' Billie asked.

'She's inside with the police,' Chile said.

'I can prove it wasn't her,' Billie said quickly reaching for Stone's list in her pocket.

'We know it wasn't. Don't worry,' Pauline smiled. 'She's giving her statement. Come on, we'll get you a cup of tea and you can tell us all about it.'

The tea was most welcome, when at last it arrived. Everyone was fussing and clucking around her. Billie didn't seem to mind though. She hadn't slept properly in over a day. She felt oddly light.

'Bill!' It was Nancy. She rushed over to her and hugged her. 'You made me nervous! I was like a long-tailed cat in a roomful of rocking chairs!'

Pauline Gower explained how, when the met officers had arrived in the morning, they had been met by a deluge of urgent messages from Group 13 Command.

'They said two RAF pilots had arrived on a stolen Liberator and with them was a stowaway ATA cadet. Then there was the news of the bombings,' Pauline said. 'We thought you, Stone and Cummings were either killed in the destruction or were under the rubble.'

'Cummings is,' Billie said in a matter-of-fact way. The adults leaned in as she explained how he was the ringleader, how he'd been in touch with the enemy and been crushed when he had run to the plane he wanted to steal. The adults couldn't disguise their outrage. Nancy looked fit to punch someone.

Billie had begun to talk in detail about the gold when Pauline cleared her throat. She knew better than to allow everyone to hear top secret information. 'I've been trying to get hold of your mother, Billie, but the man in the post office says she's not back from her shift.'

'She works overnight on Wednesdays,' Billie explained. 'She usually isn't back until after lunch on Thursdays.'

'Well, I'm glad we didn't have to worry her.'

'Stone isn't here?' Billie asked.

'No, there's been no word.' Pauline looked at her hands and then back up with a forced grin on her face. 'When did you last see him?'

'We took the last two planes, all the others...' Billie winced as she remembered the machine gun fire, and the flattened hangar... 'It was Stone's idea. He wanted to try and get a radio signal out to warn Command. He wanted to save the planes.'

'Always the war hero,' Gribble said softly.

'I lost him in the muck. I didn't have radio. We were flying echelon and we hit cloud,' Billie said sadly. 'I searched for him for ages but I was out over the sea and had to find land.'

'Flying echelon without radio!' Fairweather exclaimed. 'Rather you than me.'

'How did you make it back?' Nancy asked. 'You left from Leuchars, that's much further north than Prestwick. Prestwick is as far as I'd dare fly a fighter from here. And you got lost in the North Sea... I'm shocked you had enough fuel. That must be over four hundred miles!'

'The second tank read empty when I was over Reading,' Billie admitted. 'It probably helped that the plane is a PR, lightweight with no guns or armour...'

'Flying on fumes!' agreed Fairweather. 'The wind wasn't even with you.'

'Or the weather!' Nancy said. 'We've been grounded all morning. I got here by train from Southampton. The fog only started to clear half an hour ago.'

'You've got a guardian angel,' Diana said. 'You could have easily got lost in one of the storms.'

'But no word from Stone?' Billie asked

The smiles faltered on everyone's faces.

'I'm sure we will hear from him soon,' Pauline said confidently. 'It's not even midday. He probably stopped off for elevenses somewhere.'

Billie was about to point out the unlikelihood of this when Nancy came back into the room.

'You need rest,' Nancy said. 'Let me walk you home.'

'Billie,' said Gribble as she was getting up to leave. 'You can safely wager you've passed your class one.'

CHAPTER FORTY-FOUR

'That Spitfire is a spy plane. I expect it will have some important film on it,' Nancy said, jumping a pothole. 'You might have saved more than you realised.'

'Is Stone dead?'

'I hope not. Perhaps he bailed out and we've not heard from him yet.'

'Maybe he went back to fight,' Billie wondered as they turned into her road. 'His plane was armed.'

'One Spitfire against dozens of Luftwaffe? He's not that foolish…' Nancy sucked her teeth. 'If what you say is right about Cummings, well, maybe he defected. He could be in Germany right now.'

Billie shook her head. 'He didn't know Cummings was a traitor. They were both smuggling on the black market. But Stone wasn't a collaborator.'

'He'll turn up sometime.'

'Perhaps he got shot down…'

'Serve him right if he loses a leg. Then he'll be stuck in the ATA forever…'

'If he turns up.'

Two images filled Billie's mind. One of Stone's lone Spitfire lost in the fog, looping back in search of her above the hungry ocean. The other was an image of his family getting a telegram. She'd not considered his parents before. She pictured his mother sitting on her floor, like her mother had done when they got the news about Michael. Billie had caught her father crying. She'd never seen a man do that. She shivered and was suddenly very grateful she had made it back alive.

She felt so foolish. She could easily have been crushed by the nose wheel of the Liberator, or fallen out on landing. Without an oxygen mask she could have suffocated if the plane had reached a high enough altitude. She could have been cut in half by shrapnel had Stone not forced her down. Or murdered by the criminal Cummings. As for the flight home… Stone was an experienced pilot while she was a complete novice. He had given her his map. It seemed unfair that it was her feet plodding onto the crumbling tarmac and not his.

'I don't think I'll fly again,' Billie said.

'Hold your horses, what makes you say that?'

'I should be dead, not Stone,' Billie whispered.

Nancy wheeled round and looked Billie in the face. 'Don't ever think that! You can't bargain with death. It takes us all when it chooses. Throwing away your pilot's licence won't bring anyone back. Besides, Stone could still be alive. So less of this "I won't fly again" nonsense.'

'Even if I wanted to, they aren't going to let me! I let everyone believe I was older than I am. I missed school…'

Nancy waved her hands. 'You've done more learning at the airfield than you would have done anywhere.'

'I still lied.' Nancy rubbed her shoulder and the heavy hand gave Billie a surge of comfort. 'How am I going to tell Mum? She won't ever let me out of the house again. Let alone to the airfield.'

'After she hears what a hero you've been there is no way she won't let you back.' Nancy smiled. 'I'll drag the air marshal out here myself to talk some sense into her if I have to.'

Billie coughed a laugh but remembered the firm talking to she'd been given yesterday. 'Miss Gower won't let me fly again.'

'Sure she will,' Nancy said adamantly. 'Once you turn fourteen and are done with school.'

Billie looked horrified. 'If this war isn't over by 1944, I think the world might end.'

'We'll find a way to keep flying after the war.' Nancy smiled. 'People will still want planes delivered.'

It felt so nice to have someone on your side, backing you up. Billie felt herself well up with happiness. It was the same feeling of comfort she got when she stroked Susan.

Nancy continued to imagine the future. 'Until then, you can go back to school and spend your weekends with me in the Anson, or Ralph will always need a helping hand. Where are you going?'

'Round the back,' Billie said, making her way quickly towards the chicken coop.

Nancy put her hands on her hip and watched as Billie, using the apple tree as support, climbed on top of the garden wall. She walked like an acrobat along the top with her arms stretched out.

'Careful up there!' Nancy called.

Billie walked quickly on the mossy stones and reached the top of the outhouse. It was the old outside toilet that her father used to store his tools. Surrounding the roof was what she had glimpsed from the Spitfire.

A thick white line filled the guttering. It had looked like snow from the plane. Only it wasn't a line, or indeed snow. She grabbed her find and held it up for Nancy to see.

'Chicken eggs?' Nancy said.

'Dozens of them!' Billie beamed. 'Ha!'

'How did they get up there?'

'Susan,' Billie said, handing them down to her, one by one.

'She's been laying her eggs in the gutter? How did *she* get up there?'

'If there is one thing about the girls in this family,' boasted Billie, 'it is that they are much better at flying than people realise.'

EPILOGUE

Coop Cottage
Waltham Rd
White Waltham
Berks

1st June 1944

Dear Mrs Roosevelt,

I don't suppose you remember me but on your visit to England in 1942 you visited the ATA at White Waltham airfield and challenged me to get my pilot's licence before I turned fifteen.

When I was twelve, I went on a bit of an adventure. I've signed the Official Secrets Act or I would tell you more about it. I'm pleased to say I did rather well and, when I left school this summer, I was granted an official flight test. I met your challenge. I passed.

Yesterday I was fitted for my own uniform in London. Tomorrow I will fly the Swordfish and Tiger Moths to and from the main flight school in Thame to be serviced. All this is down to your kind words. You might also have heard that the ATA women are now paid the same as the men, and the more experienced of us are flying four-engined bombers like the Avro Lancaster.

Things seem to be picking up here. There are more of your countrymen here than ever before; more aircraft too and we are all in fits of anticipation as to what might be happening. I can't say more by letter obviously but all our prayers are with your husband and his generals. Once this beastly war is over, I hope to be reunited with my brother.

We have lost so many kind people. Friends have either gone missing or passed away (most recently dear Douglas Fairweather who I think you met when you were here) but I personally have gained considerably. All down to women like you, and your kindness and encouragement.

Thank you.

Yours sincerely,

Miss Billie Swift

CLASSIFIED INFORMATION

CONFIDENTIAL

Glossary

ATA (Air Transport Auxiliary) A civilian organisation employed by the British Government. From 1940–1945 the ATA had 1,082 male pilots, 168 female pilots and around 3000 other staff. They flew 147 different types of aircraft and pilots were expected to ferry planes they had never flown before.

BOAC (British Overseas Airways Corporation) British state-owned airline created in 1939 for ferrying civilian passengers around the world during the war, often under enemy fire.

OS maps (Ordinance Survey maps) These are special maps which mark not only the roads and towns, but the rivers, railways and even the height of the hills and mountains. During the war maps were a closely guarded resource. The fear was that enemy spies could use them to navigate. For the same reason all road signs and railway station signs were taken down.

POW (Prisoner of War) Troops who were captured by the enemy were held in camps. Most countries had signed up to the Geneva Convention of 1929 which made it illegal to torture, starve or murder prisoners of war. A lot of soldiers tried to escape. Some countries, like Russia, hadn't signed the convention so the Nazis treated their prisoners worse than the other Allied troops. The Japanese famously ran incredibly cruel camps where extremely sick men were forced to work. There were also camps for enemy POWs in Britain.

RAF (Royal Air Force) The world's oldest independent national air force. Its combined tactics of using fighters and radar in the Battle of Britain helped to stop the Nazi invasion. Later bombing of Nazi-occupied Europe, as well as ships, aided the war effort and D-Day landings. Cities like Dresden were target of destruction by Allied air forces, and there are still debates as to whether the advances in the war were worth the horrific cost to human life.

WAAF (Women's Auxiliary Air Force) Women in the RAF were not allowed to fly the planes. However, they provided crucial support services such as communications, parachute packing, meteorology, plotters in operation, and radar. Unlike in the ATA, where women were paid equal to men from 1943, they were paid 2/3 of the men's wages.

WRNS (Women's Royal Naval Service) Women in the navy were not on board fighting ships, but provided necessary services like communications and radar scanning. Wrens were also the support staff at Bletchley Park which was responsible for breaking the Nazi Enigma code.

TOP SECRET

Real Personnel

Diana Barnato Walker (1918–2008) British. Survived many exciting incidents of her own (some documented in this book). After D-Day, she regularly smuggled tins of chocolate into Belgium in her parachute bag. She used the money to go dancing and bought un-rationed sweets and leather goods. She became the fastest woman in the world in 1963, when she flew an Electric Lightning at Mach 1.65 (1968 km/h).

Clementine Churchill (1885–1977) British. Married Winston Churchill in 1908. During the war she helped many charities and was chairperson of the Red Cross Aid to Russia fund, which assisted Russians with the deprivations caused by the Nazi invasion.

Lettice Curtis (1915–2014) British. She passed her exams on four-engined bombers in 1943 which allowed other women to follow suit. Post-war, she became a senior flight development engineer. She loved air racing, helped found the British Women Pilots' Association, and in 1992 (at the age of 77) qualified to fly helicopters.

Elizabeth (Betty) Drewry (1919–????) British. She was an ATA mechanic who, in November 1943, stowed away to Canada in a Liberator in the exact same way Billie does in this book. After narrowly escaping deportation, she travelled illegally to Russia by hiding in a lifeboat. All she wanted was to learn how to fly.

Margot Duhalde aka 'Chile' (1920–2018) Chilean. She lied about her age, obtaining her flying licence before she was 18. After the war, she flew for the French air force as their first female pilot and later returned to Chile where she opened a flight school and became the first female air traffic controller in the country. She was appointed Colonel of the Chilean Air Force. She retired at 81 years old.

Prince Suprabhat Chirasakti of Siam, now known as Thailand (1917–1941). He was a cousin of the King of Siam and died when he flew his Hurricane into a hill in bad weather near Langholm, Scotland, after leaving Kirkbride. His family lived near White Waltham.

John Oliver Death (dates unknown) British. Assistant Ops Officer from January 1941 until October 1945.

Pauline Gower (1910–1947) British. Founded the women's section of the ATA. In 1943, her petitioning achieved equal pay for female pilots. This was the first time the British government gave its blessing to equal pay for equal work within an organisation under its control. Pauline died in childbirth in 1947. Her twin sons survived.

Douglas Fairweather (1890–1944) British. Joined the ATA in 1940 with his wife, Margaret. ATA pilots were supposed to carry a map for navigation: Fairweather carried a tiny one torn from the back of a pocket diary. The story of him using cigarettes for navigation is true, but he wasn't one of the pilots who made the run to Ireland for the Christmas turkeys. On 3 April 1944, Douglas was asked to transport a wounded Canadian soldier from Prestwick to White Waltham. The weather was bad and they never arrived. Later Douglas's body was washed up on the shore near Dunure. His wife, Margaret Fairweather, died the same year when her fuel tank read full but was empty. She made a forced landing and while her passengers survived, she died due to injury. Diana Barnato claimed her glasses smashed and pierced her brain through her eyes.

Herbert Greaves (1920–????) Jamaican. In 1943, US soldiers demanded Herbert be thrown out of the Casino Club in Warrington because he was black. The club owner, Nat Bookbinder, was pressured by Captain A.G. Laing of the US Army to ban all 'coloured people'. Nat said he would rather ban Americans. The Americans stopped all military personnel, including British personnel, from attending Nat's club. Nat couldn't get an answer in Parliament as to why the British joined in on the boycott. Nat was also banned from his own club when he was drafted into the British Army that same year. It shut down. We don't know what happened to Herbert but it was down to contributions like his that in the late 1940s the British Government decided to allow all British subjects entry to the UK. The first ship that landed on Tilbury docks in 1948, bringing 300 people to their new home, was called HMT Empire Windrush. From 1948 to 1955, 18,000 people came to live in Britain from the Caribbean.

William Gribble (dates unknown) British. Instructor at the ATA, previously at BOAC.

Amy Johnson (1903–1941) British. The first woman to fly solo from London to Australia. She established more flying records and was a household name. She even had a haircut named after her: the Amy Johnson wave. She died delivering an Airspeed Oxford after getting lost in bad weather, and unwittingly bailing out into the Thames Estuary and drowning.

Stewart Keith-Jopp (1891–1956) British. Lost an arm and an eye flying in WWI and was classified unfit by the RAF in WWII. He was one of three one-armed pilots who served in the ATA (the others were R.A. Corrie and Charles Dutton).

Anna Leska (1910–1998) Polish. Escaped Poland by stealing a plane from a field airport occupied by Nazis. One of three Polish female pilots who flew for the ATA.

Diana Ramsay aka 'Wamsay' (1918–1952) Australian. She survived a terrible Tempest crash when her throttle jammed. Her biggest fear was cows.

Eleanor Roosevelt (1884–1962) American. First Lady of the USA, 1933–1945. She was a controversial First Lady due to her outspokenness, particularly on civil rights for African Americans and working rights for women. She really did visit White Waltham on 26 October 1942 and gave that exact speech.

Jackie Sorour (later Moggridge) (1922–2004) South African. Learnt to fly at just 15. At 17, she was the first woman to do a parachute jump in South Africa. She came to get her advanced flying licence in the UK and stayed when war broke out. She continued being a pilot after the war.

Commander Philip Wills (1907–1978) British. Record-breaking glider pilot and second in command at the ATA. He also did a few jobs for the RAF – testing if enemy wooden gliders were detectable by British radar. Cleverly avoided crashing into a cliff by using his knowledge of 'ridge lift'.

Winkie – a type of pigeon known as a blue chequered hen, no. NEHU 40 NSL. Won the Dickin Medal in 1943 for assisting in the rescue of the aircrew of a Bristol Beaufort after it crashed in the North Sea on 23 February. She alerted the airbase at RAF Leuchars in Fife. The airbase never suffered the heavy bombing as described in this book. However, the ball bearing run is real. Gold and passengers were transported to and from Sweden in disguised Mosquitoes from Leuchars airbase.